A BAD FELINE

A WHISKERS AND WORDS MYSTERY
BOOK NINE

ERYN SCOTT

Welcome to Button
BOBBIN RD.
PATTERN DR.
Jr. High
YARD RD.
Elem.
2
BIAS RD.
RIBBON RD.
NEEDLE ST.
High School
STITCH ST.
SPOOL AVE.
SPOOL AVE.
7
12
Antiques
3
9
BBQ
4 1
THIMBLE DR.
8
THREAD LN.
THREAD LN.
10
5
PATTERN DR.
PIN ST.
Police
Pizza
6
Vet Clinic
13
Outdoor Eq.
BINDING ST.
LINEN DR.
YARD RD.
Theater
Hospital
Grocery Store
11
TEXTILE RD.
NEEDLE ST.
Button Lake
HEM AVE.
Auto Repair
Hardware
Lumber
Storage
1 - Whiskers and Words
2 - Willow's Nursery
3 - Button Bistro
4 - Scoop O' Button
5 - George's Technology Emporium
6 - Bean and Button Coffeehouse
7 - Willow and Easton's houses
8 - Material Girls
9 - The Upholstered Button
10 - Old Mansion
11 - Bank
12 - Pet Store
13 - Bakery

CHAPTER I

Despite the frigid February temperatures outside, a warmth spread through Louisa Henry as the sun dipped below the horizon. Her friends were gathered at her kitchen table, surrounded by books and brown paper. Just an hour before, the stack of books she needed to wrap for her Blind Date with a Book table for Valentine's Day at her bookshop had been overwhelming. Now, with the help of Willow and George, everything seemed manageable.

She'd planned to work on the wrapping project that night when her friends left after their weekly girls' night. But the two women had taken one look at the stacks sitting in Lou's apartment and had offered to help. Lou had immediately moved the troop of rescue cats, who called her bookshop home, downstairs so they wouldn't impede the wrapping process—some of them found the crinkly paper too tempting. Once the cats were taken care of, Lou began prepping some snacks in the kitchen, figuring keeping her friends fed was the least she could do as they helped her.

"Lou, why are you staring at us like you're about to cry?"

Willow's tone was level, the only sharpness coming from an edge of concern.

Lou shook her head, not wanting to cause her friend to worry. "No tears. I promise." She stopped cutting up fruit to swipe a finger under each eye and prove it came away dry. "I was just feeling incredibly grateful. This was supposed to be a relaxing girls' night, and here you two are, helping me wrap books."

George cut off another piece of butcher paper from the giant roll they were working from. "You needed help. That's what gals do for one another, especially on Galentine's Day."

"George," Willow dragged her name out, punctuating it with a chuckle. "What did we say about calling this Galentine's Day?"

"*You* said not to call our girls' night Galentine's Day, but *I* never agreed." She smirked wickedly. "I'm spending time with my gal pals, and it's the week before Valentine's Day. I think it's completely warranted." She bounced her thin shoulders in a shrug.

"And the fact that we do this pretty much every Tuesday?" Willow asked.

"Means we get to call next week Galentine's Day too!" George grinned.

Lou watched the exchange from the kitchen, nowhere near as upset about the term as Willow obviously was. The exasperated look Willow fixed Lou with a moment later confirmed her frustration about that fact.

"You want to back me up, Louisa? Or are you going to leave me to fight this battle alone?"

Lou put up her hands. "Hey, if she's going to help me prep

for Valentine's Day in the shop, I'd say she can rename our Tuesday night get-togethers to whatever she wants."

Willow let out a groan of complaint before muttering something about being outnumbered. "Two against one, yet again."

Knowing she and George rarely teamed up against Willow, Lou figured her friend's grumbling had to be about something else.

"Are those new renters still giving you problems?" Lou guessed. She placed the last pieces of fruit in between crackers, nuts, cheese, and olives on the large plate and brought everything over to the table.

When Willow and her significant other, Easton, had moved in together the previous month, it had been a joyous occasion. Even though the move wasn't far since Easton lived next door to Willow, it had felt like an important step. They'd been eager to rent out Easton's house … at first, but the task had grown into more of a headache than either of them had expected.

"Problems is a *generous* way to describe what the new renters are giving me." The laugh that followed Willow's statement was devoid of humor.

George flinched at the sound. "Really? I thought you were excited for them to move in. What's been going on?"

A grand inhale preceded Willow's answer to that question. "*Well,*" she started, popping an olive into her mouth before continuing. "First, it was the daily calls for one of us to come over to check the breaker box, since Micah claimed the power kept flipping on him. Then he seemed to spread out his computer equipment enough that it stopped happening, but then it was them calling us over because they swore it sounded like the dishwasher was leaking. Neither Easton nor I could find a single leak.

Rachel's the biggest problem, though. She's apparently very upset with the loudness of everything in the house. As an *actress"* —Willow said the word in a haughty voice that made Lou sure that was how Rachel had said it—"she has to make casting videos for movies and commercials and everything is too loud. She can hear it in the background of her videos. I've told her I don't know how to get rid of the sound the refrigerator makes, nor can I do anything to make the forced-air heating system sound less 'blowy.'" Willow used finger quotes around the last word, as if Lou and George might've mistaken it for her own.

George blinked at the immense amount of information Willow had just spilled. She turned to the food, making herself a stack of cheese and fruit on one of the crackers.

"And that's all in only fourteen days." Willow let her head fall forward. "I don't know how I'm going to manage six months of this."

"Thank goodness you talked Easton down from a year-long lease," Lou said. She'd stayed quiet during Willow's explanation, having heard much of the story already.

Willow let out a snort of approval. "Tell me about it. He thanks me every day. I'm not the only one having to deal with them. He goes over there just as much as I do. The only silver lining to this whole month is Quincy."

"The guy you just hired?" George squinted one eye.

Valley Nursery had operated fairly well with Willow, Peggy Lee Milton, and Beau, the young man who lived and worked at Milton Farm. But when a man had stopped by the nursery to see if she needed help on a day that she'd been trying to get everything covered for a late January snowstorm, she'd jumped at the chance to hire him.

"Yeah, he's great, and having him there means I can leave without having to close the whole place down."

A buzzing filled the apartment. Willow's body tensed as her gaze locked on to her ringing phone. It vibrated across Lou's table. Her face paled.

"It's *them*." Her voice was a frayed whisper.

"Who?" George ducked, then looked over each shoulder until Willow showed her the phone. "Oh, your renters. Do you think they heard us talking about them?" She tried to hide it, but Lou caught the note of panic in George's tone.

"Don't answer it, Willow," Lou said firmly. "They can leave a message. You've been more than attentive. You need a night off."

Muscles in her throat tensing, Willow swallowed and let the call go to voicemail. She finally exhaled when the phone stopped buzzing. "Okay, let's talk about something else. My issues are too stressful." She released a strained laugh and looked at George. "What's going on in your life?"

It was George's turn to go taut. Her gaze slid toward Lou in a plea for backup.

"George's life is ... complicated at the moment," Lou answered for her.

But Willow wasn't going to allow them to brush past her question. "Yeah, exactly, which is why she obviously needs to talk about it."

Lou met George's eyes and bounced her shoulders in a nonverbal question. *Maybe it'll be easier to just tell her?*

George seemed to agree, because she said, "I'm in the middle of trying to fall out of feelings for someone."

Lou was proud of the succinct way the young woman had described the situation.

"What's that supposed to mean?" Willow complained, obviously not finding George's word choice as eloquent as Lou did.

"It means that I have feelings for a person I shouldn't, and I'm actively working on not feeling that way about them. It's harder than you'd think," George said.

Forehead wrinkling, Willow huffed. "Someone you shouldn't? What is this, medieval times? You're allowed to have feelings for whoever you feel like having feelings for." She realized how confusing that sounded after it came out. "You know what I mean."

"George is *allowed* to have feelings for anyone, yes," Lou explained, trying to come to her friend's aid. "But she is of the impression that this person wouldn't be good for her, so she's trying to head off the feelings so she doesn't get into a situation she's not comfortable with or become someone she's not happy being."

"Okaaay." Willow pursed her lips. "I still don't get it."

"I like Wesley, okay?" George spat out the sentence.

Willow's head jutted back in recognition. They all knew the local private investigator with the blasé attitude and fluffy blond hair.

George groaned. "I like him despite the terrible first date we had, where we both decided that we weren't compatible. I like him even though he's a terrible flirt and the most infuriating man I've ever met. I like him, and I shouldn't because he made it very clear that he doesn't like me," she said, more quietly that time. Quickly, George added, "And I'm not one of those people who will chase after someone, changing who they are in the hope that the other person might return the feelings once they do. I refuse to be," she said forcefully.

"Yikes. You know I'm on your side, right?" Willow balked as if George's anger was directed at her.

George's tense body relaxed. "Sorry, I'm just on edge. Like I said, working against my feelings has been a lot more emotionally taxing than I thought it would be."

Pressing her mouth into a thin line, Lou said, "Oh, Willow knows all about pretending she doesn't have feelings for someone."

Willow gasped in surprise, but there was a playful smile on her lips. "Louisa Henry," she scolded, "you're one to talk."

Lou laughed. "You're right. I deserved that. We both fought hard against the relationships we're in now." She turned to George, who was looking rather like she'd just swallowed a bug. "*Not* that we're saying you're eventually going to be with Wesley," she added quickly.

Willow whipped her head from side to side in support of Lou's statement. "No. Not at all. Lou never hated Noah, and I only pretended to hate Easton. You truly despise Wesley. You'll be fine." Despite her supportive statement, Willow didn't sound confident. As if she realized that fact, she started wrapping another book to give herself something to do.

They all jumped as Willow's phone began vibrating across the table once more.

"Ugh. Just let me have one night of peace," Willow snapped at the phone, pressing the button to send the call straight to voicemail. Once that was done, she exhaled, lowered her shoulders, and smiled sweetly. "Where were we?"

"Well, you've dished about your problems, and I explained my miserable situation, so now it's Lou's turn." George swung her attention to Lou, who considered the prompt.

Taking a moment to write a few adjectives and tropes on

the wrapped cover of the book in front of her, Lou asked, "Would you both hate me if I said that I don't have any complaints in my life right now?"

Willow appraised her friend. "We could never hate you, Lou. We love that you're problem free."

"Absolutely. You deserve it." George nodded in agreement. "Just because the two of us are deeply troubled doesn't mean you have to be."

They laughed, each taking a break from book wrapping to eat a cracker piled with cheese and a slice of pear.

"But seriously, other than getting the shop ready for Valentine's Day, which is more fun than stressful, I can't complain about anything." Lou plucked another book from the pile, peeling off the sticky note she'd attached to the cover so she'd know what to write to give the customers an idea of what the book was about after it was wrapped: its cover and summary hidden away.

George uncapped a marker and began writing the words on the book she'd just finished wrapping. "You and Noah seem to be doing well."

Lou beamed. Next week would mark six months together—even though two of those months had been in secret, she felt they still counted. "We are. I mean, he's been a little stressed because his landlord wants to sell the house he's renting. She's given him the choice to either buy it or move out at the end of his lease."

"Huh, it's like the opposite of Willow's problem tenants," George said with a chuckle. "Noah's got a problem landlord."

Willow snorted, but turned to Lou. "And he doesn't want to buy it? I thought he loved that house."

"He does," Lou confirmed. "It was perfect for what he and

Marigold needed in the years since the divorce, but he said he always pictured settling in a place with a little more land."

"The houses in his neighborhood are definitely a lot closer than I'd like to be with my neighbors." Willow creased the paper as she wrapped another book.

"Exactly." Lou sighed. "Which means he might be on the lookout for a new home in the coming weeks."

"Or he could stay here with you." George waggled her eyebrows at her.

A smile shone on Lou's face before she could stop it. "I've thought about that. It might be a little cramped with Marigold here half the time, though. We could make it work for a while, but Cassidy says the housing market is really tough for buyers right now. Places are getting snapped up within the first few days, and she's had clients who've been searching for six months or more."

Willow opened her mouth to say something, but her phone began buzzing again, causing her to clamp her lips shut as she let out a strangled groan.

"Again?" George asked with a grimace.

"Yes." Willow clamped her eyes shut tight, as if that might make her invisible.

Lou gulped, regretting her earlier suggestion that Willow ignore the calls. "Three calls in a row? Are you sure you shouldn't just answer it, Willow? It might be an emergency."

Letting out an exasperated groan, Willow said, "You're right. Plus, Easton's working late tonight, and I don't want them bothering him when they can't get ahold of me." Sucking in a steadying breath, Willow answered the call. "Rachel. Hi." Her tone was firm and cold. Any hardness to her features softened as she listened. "The horse *and* the goat? Are you sure?"

Her gaze flicked up to Lou and George. Worry built behind her blue-gray eyes. "Okay, I'll be right there to check things out. Thank you for letting me know. Yes, sorry you had to call so many times. Okay, I'll let you know."

George and Lou leaned forward as Willow ended the call, waiting to hear what was going on.

"Rachel says OC and Steve are making a bunch of noise in the barn. She said OC keeps kicking at the wall."

"Which he only does when he's aggravated," Lou said, having known the horse his whole life.

"Right. And she said Steve's been screaming just as long."

"Which *he* only does when there's someone around who he doesn't know," George supplied, having been on the receiving end of the goat's bleating cries before.

Willow was already on her feet. "I'm going to check it out and make sure they're okay."

Lou stood just as Willow reached for her purse. "We'll come with you."

"Yeah, I could use a field trip." George pushed back from the table.

With the cats downstairs, Lou wouldn't have to worry about them getting into the food. But she wasn't sure how long they would be gone, so she moved their plate of snacks to the fridge.

Once the food was put away, the three of them piled into Willow's car and headed down Thread Lane. It was odd for Lou to see anything but Easton's sedan parked in front of the gray house next to Willow's. But she couldn't concentrate too much on the neighbors because the moment Willow parked, she rushed out of the car and disappeared around to her backyard, where a small barn was located. Lou and George raced after her.

A loud hammering rang through the otherwise quiet night. Then it stopped, followed by an annoyed snort from OC, Willow's chestnut gelding. The silence was short-lived as Steve filled it with a panicked bleat.

The trio of women rushed into the barn, but a gray pygmy goat stopped them short. He wore pink pajamas with hearts on them. It looked like George wasn't the only one getting in the Valentine's Day spirit.

But while the goat's pajamas should've been cute, a few extra splotches of red told a different story. Those red spots were definitely not in the shape of hearts.

It was blood.

Willow loosed a strangled cry as she peered past the goat and saw a stranger lying in the middle of the small barn. There was a knife sticking out of his chest.

"Steve, what did you do to that man?" George asked quietly.

CHAPTER 2

George had her phone out within seconds and had called Easton before Lou could so much as blink. Seeing that George had that part of emergency protocol under control, Lou concentrated on Willow.

Her best friend ran over to the man in the middle of the barn, kneeling next to him to check for a pulse. But even before she could touch his wrist, Willow balked at the body. Lou raced to her side, wondering if the knife in his chest wasn't the only horrific part of the scene.

She found the man's face untouched and unfamiliar.

Glancing back at Willow, who'd turned as pale as snow, she came to the only other conclusion, given her friend's reaction. "Do you know him?"

Just because Lou didn't recognize the man didn't mean her friend wouldn't.

Proving Lou's point, Willow moved her head up and then down, the gesture painfully slow. She finally found her voice, croaking out, "Do you remember a few weeks ago, when I told you about the potential renter Easton and I met with? The one who gave us both such a bad feeling?"

Lou did. "He was asking about your schedules as if he might rob you while the two of you were at work." She cut a glare toward the body. "That's him?"

Willow only gulped in response.

"Maybe he came back to do the job even though he didn't get the rental." Lou's attention swept over the rest of the barn, searching for clues or signs of a burglary. "But if he was here to steal from you, who killed *him*?"

The two women turned to look at the small goat standing next to George. Then they turned their inquiring gazes on the horse, still safely in his stall.

As if Willow just remembered that both animals had been making quite the ruckus, she sprinted toward Steve, scooping him into her arms as she checked for any injuries. Once she was convinced the blood on his pajamas was, in fact, not his own, she flung open the stall door and performed the same checks on OC.

"They're both fine," Willow said, the sentence encased in a relieved exhale. She exited the stall, sliding the door closed behind her. She locked the latch and slumped her weight back against the door.

George moved closer to Willow, either in support or to distance herself from the body. "Sorry, did I hear you say you know who this guy is?"

Seeing Willow was out of words, Lou was about to answer for her, but someone else beat her to it.

"He applied to rent my house about a month ago," Easton said as he stepped into the barn, opening his arms preemptively as Willow raced toward him. "And he gave both of us the creeps, so we turned down his application." The tendons in Easton's neck tightened as he observed the dead man, nodding toward the body when the other officers caught up.

He stayed put, squeezing Willow tighter to him until his presence steadied her enough that she could stand up straight once more. He kept an arm wrapped around her shoulders as the officers confirmed the man was dead and began searching for clues.

"Steve has blood on his pjs," Willow whispered, breaking the silence as the officers worked. "When we first arrived, it kinda looked like he was the one who'd stabbed the guy," she added with a slightly unhinged cackle.

Easton's lips twitched downward. "I thought you were at Lou's tonight. How'd you know to come here?"

"Rachel called three times in a row." Despite the terrible way the evening had turned out, Willow still managed to squeeze out enough sass to throw an eye roll over her shoulder toward their rental house. "I finally picked up, and she told me Steve was screaming his head off, and OC was kicking his stall. We came to check it out and found..." She gestured toward the man.

"Can I inspect the goat, Willow?" Officer Givens asked, having overheard their conversation.

Willow opened the stall for him, picking up Steve and handing him over to the officer, who reacted like he'd been handed a baby but didn't know how to hold one.

While Officer Givens checked over the goat, Easton entered the stall and approached OC. He ran a gentle hand down the length of the horse's long nose, murmuring something into his soft ears. OC huffed a breath out of his nostrils and then settled his head against Easton's chest. The detective reached forward to pat the horse's neck.

Lou remembered back when Easton had pretended to hate that horse, using its constant break-out attempts as a reason to complain to Willow when, in reality, he'd merely wanted an excuse to talk to her. Easton and OC were now the best of friends.

More officers entered the barn. "No one in Willow's house. No signs of forced entry. You'll know better than us whether anything's missing, but we didn't see any signs of a burglary."

The officers must've split off from the group that had come directly to the barn.

Easton told them thanks and turned to Willow. "I let them inside on our way by the house to make sure whoever did this hadn't gone inside too."

Willow ran her hands up and down her arms.

"Easton, we've got something over here," Officer Reynolds called as Willow and Givens replaced the goat into the stall. Reynolds held up a gloved hand, clutching a piece of paper he'd extracted from the dead man's pocket.

Heading in that direction, Easton craned his neck so his head matched the angle of the paper. He squinted his eyes, proving that the handwriting was either difficult to decipher or whatever written there was concerning. Based on the way Easton's face drained of color, his throat bobbing with a hard swallow, Lou guessed it was the latter.

Sensing the same thing, Willow rushed to his side, poring over the text. She let out a ragged breath. "He was tracking your movements?" The question was tight, as if Willow was trying her hardest not to be sick.

"For the past three weeks, it appears." Easton's posture stiffened. "And not just mine. Yours too."

Willow's hand moved to her chest as she read, "Tuesday nights—Willow gone—girls' night."

Fear trickled down Lou's spine, adding to the shiver she felt coming on because of the cold. But her reaction was nothing close to the obvious panic Willow experienced seeing their movements mapped out like that.

"I *knew* I got a bad feeling about him," Willow said with an exaggerated shiver. "He obviously knew I would be gone tonight and took advantage of the fact that you stayed late at the station so he could break in."

"Then who did this?" Givens pointed to the knife, repeating the question Lou had brought up before law enforcement arrived.

Easton rubbed a hand over the base of his neck. "If we're not his first attempted burglary, he could have enemies," Easton offered. "Maybe one of them followed him here, and his death in our barn is merely a coincidence." The detective shrugged, but froze in the middle of the movement. "Is that a tattoo?" He motioned to the dead man's right wrist.

Givens knelt next to the body and used his gloved hand to inch the man's jacket sleeve up enough that a tattoo became visible. "Looks like a cobra," he said, glancing up. "Did he have that when you interviewed him a few weeks ago?"

Willow and Easton shared an indecisive look.

"He was wearing long sleeves," Willow said. "I didn't notice."

Easton confirmed he hadn't either. Looking around the barn, the detective appeared to be at a loss for what to do next.

It was the first time since she'd met him that Lou had ever seen him so affected by a crime scene.

Officer Givens was less distressed, thankfully. He stood, dusting off his uniform. "If he's got a record, we'll figure out who he is and why he was here. Don't you worry about it."

Givens directed the crime scene team to check the place for any more clues before they dusted for fingerprints. As the detective in charge, that responsibility should've fallen to Easton. But that was the nice thing about living in a small town like Button; the officers weren't just coworkers but neighbors and friends. Givens likely knew that Easton would need support when it came to a murder on his property. And with the way local officers respected Easton, none of them minded stepping up to help in a situation like this. Even the notoriously ornery Officer Reynolds was being helpful.

Proving she was keeping a slightly more level head than her significant other about the situation, Willow asked, "Should we go through the house and check for missing items?"

The way she studied Easton told Lou that Willow's suggestion was more about giving him some space to think rather than being worried any of their possessions might be missing.

As Easton nodded, and Willow led him toward the house, her eyes landed on Lou and George. "Oh, I should drive the two of you home first. Sorry, I forgot we took my car here."

"Don't worry about us," George told her.

"Yeah," Lou said. "We can walk back."

Officer Givens got to his feet. "Actually, I need to run by the station to grab a fingerprinting kit since we came here in such a rush. I can drop you two off on my way."

George and Lou thanked him, hugging Willow and Easton

before following the officer to his patrol car parked haphazardly in Willow's driveway. Buckled in, Lou exhaled the worst of her worries, but something told her the more they learned about what happened to the man in Willow's barn, the more their February—like Steve's pajamas—was about to be less about love and more about murder.

CHAPTER 3

Officer Givens dropped George off first, looping around toward Whiskers and Words on his way back toward the police station.

"Thanks," Lou said as she climbed out of the warm cruiser and rushed for the shop door, her frigid fingers gripping her keys.

She rushed inside after unlocking the door, ready to spend a few minutes in front of the fireplace upstairs. But as she moved farther into the bookshop, a noise stopped her. At that moment, she remembered she'd moved the cats to the bookshop so they wouldn't bother the wrapping operation upstairs.

But something much larger than a cat created the scraping sound Lou heard next.

Her keys jangled as her fingers shook. Was she being paranoid because of the crime scene she'd just left? Or was it possible that someone had broken into the bookshop while she'd been gone?

There was another scratching sound, and then a small crash came from her office in the back of the bookshop. Lou's chest tightened, and for a terrifying moment, she couldn't pull enough breath into her lungs. Then her rational mind took over. If someone had broken in, there would be signs of forced entry. There were none as far as she could see.

She was about to check the back door when Anne Mice came rushing out from the office. The fur on her nape stood up in wet clumps.

"What did you get into?" Lou asked as the gray tabby slunk past her.

"Lou?" Noah's deep voice rang through the quiet, empty bookshop.

Her heart settled, lungs relaxing enough to let her take a deep breath. "Hey, Noah," she said when her significant other stepped out of the office. "What are you doing here?"

He ran a hand through his almost black hair. "Sorry, I know you were supposed to have your girls' get-together tonight, but I forgot it was flea medicine day for the cats, and I didn't want to miss it. I was trying to be quiet down here so I wouldn't bug the three of you, but I guess I didn't need to worry. You weren't even here." He glanced between the front door, where Lou had come from, to the apartment, where he'd expected her to be.

Lou let out an exhaled puff of air. "Yeah, we got called to Willow's for what we thought was going to be a quick trip, but it turned into something much longer."

Motioning for her to sit in the cozy seating area in the middle of the shop, Noah asked, "What happened?"

Lou explained. She told him about the three calls in a row from Willow's renter, as well as why it took her three calls to answer, and then the terrible sight they'd found once they'd gone to Willow's to investigate.

Noah covered her hand with his as he scooted closer. "So they knew the guy? Do you remember his name?"

Lou blinked. "I-I … I didn't ask that." She frowned at the realization, and Noah mirrored the gesture.

It wasn't like Lou to miss out on details like that.

"That's okay. I was just wondering if I would recognize him." Noah gave her an encouraging smile, but Lou's uncharacteristic lack of attention to detail must've clued him in to how shaken she was by the whole encounter because he said, "Annie was the last one, so I'm all done with the flea medicine. Why don't we go upstairs, and I'll make you some tea? We can start a fire and warm you up."

After the chilling night she'd had, Lou wasn't going to stop him if he wanted to take care of her. She let herself be led upstairs, and sank onto her couch while Noah turned on the fireplace and started hot water boiling.

He assessed the stack of unwrapped books. Without prompting, he sat in front of the pile Willow had been working on and began wrapping. Just as it had been with her friends, Lou's heart swelled at the sight of Noah helping her. The reminder that she was so well taken care of warmed her more than the fireplace ever could. She stood and grabbed the charcuterie board from the fridge, placing it on the table.

"Hey, I'm supposed to be taking care of you," Noah teased.

He moved past her, pouring water into the two mugs he'd prepped with tea bags. They worked in companionable silence for a few minutes before Lou felt like herself again.

"How was your day?" she asked, realizing it had been all about her until that point.

"Nothing like a body in a barn to complain about." Noah added another wrapped book to the finished pile.

Lou glanced at him sidelong. "That doesn't mean you can't have had a bad day."

He bobbed his head. "You're right. To be honest, it wasn't great."

"More stuff with your landlord?"

"Nothing new on that front. Today it was work stress."

Lou listened intently. Kathleen, the manager of Noah's veterinary clinic, was on vacation for two weeks.

"I didn't think it was possible for me to be more appreciative of Kathleen, but this week is proving me wrong." Noah rubbed at his temples. "The person I brought in to replace her is fine, but when you're used to Kathleen, fine just doesn't cut it."

In a normal week, if Kathleen needed to take time off, Noah and the vet techs would take over her duties. But the woman loved what she did and rarely took more than a day or two off in a row. The two-week vacation she'd booked to go to California to visit her sister was something rare. Happy as Noah and the rest of the staff were that Kathleen was taking a break, it left a gap in coverage more than he and the techs could handle. Noah had hired a temporary replacement for the two weeks—with Kathleen's blessing, of course.

"I swear, I spent so much time today answering questions that it probably would've just been faster to do everything myself. It's not the temporary manager's fault, though. She's trying her best." He exhaled a whoosh of air, seeming to get over the frustration with the motion. He surveyed the finished stack of books, searching for more. "Are these part of the blind-date table?" Noah hitched a thumb toward a group of books sitting on her coffee table, ready to tackle any other jobs she needed done.

"No. Those are for a new table I'm going to try out this year. In Love with Puzzles. They're all puzzle books, and I've got some jigsaw puzzles coming tomorrow that should add to the display."

"I'm not sure if I'm in *love* with puzzles, but I like them." Noah chuckled to himself as he picked up one of the books and flipped through. "I've never heard of logic puzzles before."

"Oh!" Lou raced over to him. "I hadn't either until the books came in the other day. They're really cool. You use deductive reasoning to figure out the answers, and these grids help you keep track of the clues." She opened the page and showed Noah an example. Seeing a muscle twitch in his jaw as he examined the six-by-six-by-three grid, Lou realized that he was still confused. "Here, let me show you. I tried making my own last night so I could explain it to customers in the shop." She brought him over to the couch and grabbed the notepad she'd been working on.

"You made one yourself?" Noah stared at the complicated grid in front of him.

"It took me a few tries, but I think I figured it out." She pointed to the page.

	British Blue	Gray Tabby	White	Tortoiseshell	Orange/white	Fireplace	Loveseat	Tabletop	Under bkshelf	Lap
Sapphire										
Catnip Everdeen										
Anne Mice										
Charles Lickens										
Meatball										
Fireplace										
Loveseat										
Tabletop										
Under bkshelf										
Lap										

"Okay, so logic puzzles are usually trying to figure out relationships between people, places, and behaviors," Lou explained. "The game Clue is a great example of that. Each suspect can only have been in one room and used one weapon, so if you know Mr. Mustard had the candlestick, no one else could've had it."

Noah nodded, showing he was on the same page.

"I made mine about the cats. I used the bookshop cats, and we're figuring out what their favorite sleeping place is, as well as what color their fur is by following the clues," Lou said. "Just pretend you don't already know all of this."

Noah laughed, rubbing his hand over his face as if wiping

away the fatigue of the day. "Okay. Clue one is, 'The British Blue cat is named after someone very important to its breed's country of origin. He also maintains a very British sense of aloofness.'" He glanced over at the grid. "Okay, British Blue. British. Of the names on the list, Charles Dickens would fit that. Charles Lickens. What do I do if I know the answer?" The pen hovered over the page.

Lou tapped the square where both Charles Lickens and British Blue met. "You can either fill in the square or write an O to signify that it's a match. Most people have a different preferred way, but I would suggest *against* a check mark since it's too close to an X, and that could get confusing when you move to bigger, more difficult puzzles. The Xs come next, so let me know when you're ready."

Noah marked the square with an O. He waited once that was done.

"Okay, now that we know Charles Lickens is the British Blue, we can say that none of the other cats are British Blues, so go ahead and X out the rest of that column. And Charles isn't any of the other fur colors, so you can also X out that row."

Noah showed her once he was done.

	British Blue	Gray Tabby	White	Tortoiseshell	Orange/white	Fireplace	Loveseat	Tabletop	Under bkshelf	Lap
Sapphire	X									
Catnip Everdeen	X									
Anne Mice	X									
Charles Lickens	O	X	X	X	X					
Meatball	X									
Fireplace										
Loveseat										
Tabletop										
Under bkshelf										
Lap										

"Great. Now, if you feel you have all the information you're going to get out of that clue, I would put a line through it, so you know you don't have to come back to it." Lou tilted her head. "This puzzle's not so hard, but for the more difficult ones, that's been helping me keep track of which clues I need to go back over."

Noah crossed out the first clue, then moved on to reading the next one aloud. "'The deaf cat likes to sleep on a stack of books on the table.' I mean, I know that the white cat is most likely to be deaf, but I should probably wait on this clue until I have more information." His gaze traveled down to the third clue. "Ah, 'Sapphire is the white cat, and he unfortunately can't hear when people comment on his beautiful blue eyes.'"

Noah marked Sapphire as the white cat and the cat who sleeps on the table. He added the Xs along the rows and columns without Lou even having to remind him.

	British Blue	Gray Tabby	White	Tortoiseshell	Orange/white	Fireplace	Loveseat	Tabletop	Under bkshelf	Lap
Sapphire	X	X	O	X	X	X	X	O	X	X
Catnip Everdeen	X		X					X		
Anne Mice	X		X					X		
Charles Lickens	O	X	X	X	X			X		
Meatball	X		X					X		
Fireplace			X							
Loveseat			X							
Tabletop	X	X	O	X	X					
Under bkshelf			X							
Lap			X							

"You're an excellent student." Lou nodded in approval.

Noah winked at her and read the next one. "'Catnip Everdeen is most comfortable when she's hidden.'" He wet his lips. "Okay, this one is pretty clear. The only hidden place to sleep is under a bookshelf." He marked that as well, striking a line through that clue.

	British Blue	Gray Tabby	White	Tortoiseshell	Orange/white	Fireplace	Loveseat	Tabletop	Under bkshelf	Lap
Sapphire	X	X	O	X	X	X	X	O	X	X
Catnip Everdeen	X		X			X	X	X	O	X
Anne Mice	X		X					X	X	
Charles Lickens	O	X	X	X	X			X	X	
Meatball	X		X					X	X	
Fireplace			X							
Loveseat			X							
Tabletop	X	X	O	X	X					
Under bkshelf			X							
Lap			X							

"'Of the locations in the bookshop, the fireplace gets the least amount of foot traffic, since it's in the corner. The sitting area with the couch and love seat get the most.'" Noah's expression shifted as he contemplated that. "I think I might need to save that one. The next one says, 'The gray tabby and the British Blue often fight to be the center of attention.'" He marked the puzzle, narrating as he did. "That means neither of those cats would want to be under a bookshelf or near the fireplace, since those get the lowest amount of foot traffic. Oh, that also means that Catnip couldn't be the British Blue, which we already knew, or the gray tabby, which we didn't." He added an X where Catnip intersected with gray tabby.

	British Blue	Gray Tabby	White	Tortoiseshell	Orange/white	Fireplace	Loveseat	Tabletop	Under bkshelf	Lap
Sapphire	X	X	O	X	X	X	X	O	X	X
Catnip Everdeen	X	X	X			X	X	X	O	X
Anne Mice	X		X					X	X	
Charles Lickens	O	X	X	X	X			X	X	
Meatball	X		X					X	X	
Fireplace	X	X	X							
Loveseat			X							
Tabletop	X	X	O	X	X					
Under bkshelf	X	X	X							
Lap			X							

He moved on. "'Sapphire and Catnip are the only two cats with white fur.'" His eyebrows jumped. "So, since we already know Sapphire is completely white, that means Catnip has to be the orange and white cat. Which also means that the orange and white cat likes to be under the bookshelf."

	British Blue	Gray Tabby	White	Tortoiseshell	Orange/white	Fireplace	Loveseat	Tabletop	Under bkshelf	Lap
Sapphire	X	X	O	X	X	X	X	O	X	X
Catnip Everdeen	X	X	X	X	O	X	X	X	O	X
Anne Mice	X		X		X			X	X	
Charles Lickens	O	X	X	X	X			X	X	
Meatball	X		X		X			X	X	
Fireplace	X	X	X		X					
Loveseat			X		X					
Tabletop	X	X	O	X	X					
Under bkshelf	X	X	X	X	O					
Lap			X		X					

"Yes, and now check out that bottom set," Lou said. "Now that you've marked out those clues, what's the only cat color left available for the fireplace?"

"The tortoiseshell." Noah made the correct marks. "Oh, and I missed that, if the British Blue is Charles, he won't want to be by the fireplace, since that's out of the way."

	British Blue	Gray Tabby	White	Tortoiseshell	Orange/white	Fireplace	Loveseat	Tabletop	Under bkshelf	Lap
Sapphire	X	X	O	X	X	X	X	O	X	X
Catnip Everdeen	X	X	X	X	O	X	X	X	O	X
Anne Mice	X		X		X			X	X	
Charles Lickens	O	X	X	X	X	X		X	X	
Meatball	X		X		X			X	X	
Fireplace	X	X	X	O	X					
Loveseat			X	X	X					
Tabletop	X	X	O	X	X					
Under bkshelf	X	X	X	X	O					
Lap			X	X	X					

He read the next clue. "'Meatball is getting bolder, but she still prefers to stay out of the way, hiding much like the animal named in her coloring.' Okay, so that means Meatball is the tortoiseshell, which also means she's the fireplace cat." He smirked. "And with that clue, I know all the cat names and colors."

	British Blue	Gray Tabby	White	Tortoiseshell	Orange/white	Fireplace	Loveseat	Tabletop	Under bkshelf	Lap
Sapphire	X	X	O	X	X	X	X	O	X	X
Catnip Everdeen	X	X	X	X	O	X	X	X	O	X
Anne Mice	X	O	X	X	X	X		X	X	
Charles Lickens	O	X	X	X	X	X		X	X	
Meatball	X	X	X	O	X	O	X	X	X	X
Fireplace	X	X	X	O	X					
Loveseat			X	X	X					
Tabletop	X	X	O	X	X					
Under bkshelf	X	X	X	X	O					
Lap			X	X	X					

He drew a line through the last couple of clues. "But that's it. I still don't know where Anne Mice and Charles Lickens like to sleep."

"Don't you?" Lou tapped the very first clue. "If Charles maintains a bit of aloofness, would he sit in a customer's lap?"

"Ah, I see. He's the center of attention, but not too close. He's the love-seat guy. And Anne is on laps. Usually Forrest's," Noah added with a chuckle as he finished the puzzle.

	British Blue	Gray Tabby	White	Tortoiseshell	Orange/white	Fireplace	Loveseat	Tabletop	Under bkshelf	Lap
Sapphire	X	X	O	X	X	X	X	O	X	X
Catnip Everdeen	X	X	X	X	O	X	X	X	O	X
Anne Mice	X	O	X	X	X	X	X	X	X	O
Charles Lickens	O	X	X	X	X	X	O	X	X	X
Meatball	X	X	X	O	X	O	X	X	X	X
Fireplace	X	X	X	O	X					
Loveseat	O	X	X	X	X					
Tabletop	X	X	O	X	X					
Under bkshelf	X	X	X	X	O					
Lap	X	O	X	X	X					

"These are pretty fun. I feel like Marigold would really like them," Noah said, mentioning his inquisitive daughter.

"I was thinking the same thing." Lou motioned to the stack of logic puzzle books she'd ordered for her display. "You should take one of these books home for her, as well as a cat puzzle."

Noah did, tucking them by his jacket so he wouldn't forget them when he left. He turned to Lou. "I'll give those to her tomorrow when I pick her up from school. As for now, what else can I help you with for the upcoming event?"

While the official holiday was next Wednesday, Lou wanted to have the displays up and ready tomorrow so they'd be out for a full week leading up to the big day. She could easily set up the different displays tomorrow, now that the bulk of the work was done.

"I think that's it." She opened her arms to give him a grateful hug.

Noah stepped toward her, wrapping her up in his warmth. "Okay, then, are there any non-bookshop-related things I can do to get ready for the holiday?" He leaned back just enough to catch her eye.

"What did you have in mind?" she asked playfully.

"It's our first Valentine's Day together. I don't know whether you like to celebrate. I figured I'd check before I started making any plans."

Lou contemplated that. Her late husband, Ben, had always been big on Valentine's Day. Even when they'd been broke college students, he'd made sure to go all out on the day so she felt loved. Taking that as a cue that he would appreciate the same, Lou also went big with her plans and gifts. And while she didn't need to do anything extravagant, the thought of celebrating her love for Noah sounded like a great idea.

"Yeah," she said, repeating the sentiment more confidently the second time. "Yes, I do. You?"

Noah appeared to go through the same thought process as her, obviously going through his preferences from his past relationship. "Yes. Same." The light in his dark eyes caused Lou to melt back into his arms.

When Ben died a few years earlier, she couldn't have dreamed she'd get a chance to find love again, let alone with someone like Noah. Lou was excited to plan something that might come close to making him realize how grateful she was to have him in her life.

CHAPTER 4

Despite the lovely surprise of getting to spend a few hours with Noah that evening, Lou's thoughts returned to the body in Willow's barn as she got ready for bed. Her worries surrounding the event made sleep elusive that night.

Finally, Lou gave up trying to sleep and went for an early morning run before tackling the Valentine's Day displays in the bookshop.

"Oh, you got everything done already," George said with a pout as she entered the bookshop later that morning. "I was planning on helping with more wrapping since we got interrupted last night, but I see you finished it all."

"No worries." Lou waved a hand toward her friend. "Noah came over and helped me last night, and I set everything up this morning." She motioned to the Valentine's Day-themed table displays she'd created, pride rushing through her as she took them in.

George let her cat, Geralt, out of the carrier she put him in while she walked around town. She let him socialize with the other bookshop cats while she went toward the table Lou had set up, with the sign that had a heart made of puzzle pieces. She snapped up one of the copies of the cat logic puzzle Lou had printed out after she and Noah had parted ways the night before.

"What's this?" George's expression danced with intrigue.

From the love seat, Forrest took his nose out of the book he was reading. Even Silas put down his paper, something they heard before they saw it. The crinkling rang through the quiet shop.

"Oh, it's a grid logic puzzle." Lou gestured to the stack of books on the puzzle table and explained, "They're deductive-reasoning puzzles. I bought a few books of these for the display. They were new to me, so I figured they might be new to other people as well, and I made my own puzzle to show people how they're done using a subject matter we're all comfortable with … the cats!"

George pored over the instructions Lou had written out at the top of the page. "No Geralt?" She stuck out her bottom lip.

"He's more of an honorary bookshop cat," Lou said, eyeing the big gray cat who hated to be separated from his person so much that George carried him around in a baby sling.

Forrest rose from his place on the love seat and grabbed a copy of the puzzle. He took a second one when Silas cleared his throat and craned his neck to see what it was all about.

That was how Cricket, Lou's final regular, found them all minutes later when she bustled into the bookshop.

"What's going on here? Are you all taking a test or something?" Cricket unwound the scarf from her neck and peered at the papers they held.

George stabbed the pencil she was using toward the stack

on the display table. "It's a puzzle Lou made about the cats. It's fun." To Lou, she added, "I know a lot of this stuff from hanging around the cats, but I can see how it would be challenging if I didn't."

Lou grinned. "That's the point. They really make your brain work."

The front door opened just as Cricket reached for her own copy of the puzzle. Lou got ready to greet her first non-regular customer of the day, but found yet another friend entering the bookshop. Willow strode inside, amusement playing at the edges of her lips as the regulars worked on their puzzles.

"Morning." Lou came around the register counter to pull Willow into a tight hug. "How are you doing?"

Willow squeezed Lou back, but even that motion lacked its usual strength. "I've definitely been better. Peggy Lee made me take today off. She's running the nursery with Quincy today."

"Smart woman," Cricket called over her shoulder without taking her eyes off the logic puzzle in front of her. "It's not every day you find a dead man in your barn."

The other regulars murmured their agreement. Lou didn't even ask how they knew already. Neither she nor George had said a word.

Even though she felt like she was truly becoming a Buttonite, she would never get used to how quickly the rumor mill worked. "How are Steve and OC handling everything?"

"They're great, actually." Surprise flitted over Willow's features. "I spent hours in the barn with them last night after the crime scene crew cleared out and then gave them both a full grooming this morning. Honestly, I think they're sick of me. Which is why I've come here to hang out with you. I figured I could come help wrap books since we got interrupted last night."

Lou's heart warmed at her friend's offer, but she cringed in apology. "Actually, Noah came over, and we finished. Sorry. I'm all caught up for Valentine's Day." She indicated to the different displays around the shop as if Willow might need proof that everything had been taken care of. Seeing that her friend still appeared a little lost, Lou asked, "Any more news on the guy from the barn?"

Willow sucked in a breath. "Actually, yes. His name was Tyson Krate."

"Was that the same name he used on the rental application?" Lou asked. She could sense her regulars keeping one ear on the conversation as they worked on their logic puzzles.

"It is. Which, if you ask me, was pretty bold since he had a record." Willow exhaled a snort. "Though, we didn't find out until now since we got such a bad feeling from him, he didn't even make it to the point where we asked for any of his personal information."

Lou tensed. "Was his record for something bad?"

"Petty theft." Willow jerked her shoulders in a shrug. "Apparently, he was a bit of a pickpocket during his younger years."

"Well, based on the fact that he was most likely in your barn to rob you, it doesn't seem like he cleaned up his act in the decades since," Lou said.

Willow scoffed. "Especially since we're pretty sure he was a part of the Muscle Car Mafia."

At the name, gasps rang out from Lou's regulars, and they each abandoned their puzzles, turning to focus on Lou and Willow's conversation.

"You don't say?" Silas asked, eyes alight with intrigue.

"What's the Muscle Car Mafia?" Lou asked.

Cricket scoffed. "Lou, you fit in around here so well, I always forget how little you know."

Lou scowled at the declaration, but both Willow and George sent her calming looks that told her Cricket's statement was likely supposed to be a compliment.

"About seven years ago, the Muscle Car Mafia terrorized this part of the state, Button especially," Forrest explained. "They stole cars, either reselling them or stripping them for parts."

"And they only stole muscle cars?" Lou still didn't understand. "There can't be that many in Button."

She'd learned about Liza Osborne and her father's old Shelby Mustang in a case during her first spring in town, but hadn't seen an abundance of classic cars. Especially not enough to lure a gang of car thieves to target the town.

"A common misconception," Cricket answered. "They weren't called that because they stole muscle cars."

George inclined her head. "They were called that because they each had code names and those were all based on muscle cars."

"The code name thing started because the guy who ran the crew is legally named Chevelle." Silas rolled his eyes, as if anyone couldn't have guessed from his tone that he thought it was ridiculous.

Cricket used her fingers to count off the names. "There were six of them, seven, if you count Chevelle. Viper, Firebird, GTO, Daytona, Mustang, and…"

"Cobra," Willow answered for her.

The snake tattoo on the man's forearm last night flashed into Lou's memory. "Tyson was Cobra?"

Willow's chin descended in a solemn nod.

"But Easton was at the station, and you were at my house, so both of your cars were gone." Lou tapped her fingers on the counter. "Was he trying to steal your truck?"

Willow used her diesel truck mainly for hauling the horse trailer, so it sat largely unused in her garage during the winter months when she didn't have trail rides or horse shows to haul OC to.

"He might've been there for the truck," Willow admitted. "I guess we'll never know. He can't exactly tell us now."

Silas groaned. "I thought we were past all of that car-stealing business when Chevelle was put away."

"The boss was arrested?" Lou asked.

Everyone nodded.

"About five years ago," Willow explained. "Easton's actually the one who caught them. It's part of what helped him get his promotion to detective."

"Could this be retaliation?" Lou asked.

"Yeah," George said. "Maybe this Cobra guy was mad at Easton for putting his boss away, so he was trying to steal from him for revenge."

Willow swept her hair behind her ear. "That's what Easton thinks. As for why he's dead? That's still a mystery."

They chatted a while longer, moving on to happier subjects such as what everyone's plans were for Valentine's Day. When the bulk of Lou's regulars headed out, Willow followed despite Lou's offer for her to stay longer at the shop.

"I'll find something to do around the barn, I'm sure."

Willow waved over her shoulder as she stepped out into the chilly morning.

Lou knew Willow could always find something to do around her barn. She just hoped whatever it was would be enough to take her friend's mind off the murder that had happened in that very spot.

LATER THAT NIGHT, Lou was reading in bed when she got a text from Willow.

Hey, sorry it's so late. Are you up?

A frown etched itself into the corner of Lou's mouth, but she typed out a response.

Yeah. Everything okay?

Willow's response came through right away.

Can we come upstairs?

Lou's back-door camera alerted her to a presence in the alley behind Whiskers and Words. Willow and Easton stood there, Easton carrying a duffel bag while Willow waved at the camera.

Come on up.

Lou sent the text and then threw back the covers, hustling

over to the stairs that led into the bookshop just as Willow and Easton clomped up them.

"Is everything okay?" Lou repeated her texted question as they stopped just inside her apartment and Easton set down the duffel bag.

Willow shot Easton a look that was full of frustration, making her significant other wince. Lou's heart hammered as worry rose inside her. Were they fighting? Had they broken up? There was definitely tension between the two, and now that they had renters next door, there wasn't anywhere for them to go if they had a fight.

"We're wondering if Willow can stay with you for a few days," Easton said, quickly adding, "until I know for sure that our house is safe."

His words did nothing to assuage Lou's worries.

Seeing that Lou's mind was jumping to all the worst possible scenarios, Willow said, "Easton almost got run off the road tonight when he was on his way home from the station."

"That's awful." Lou placed a hand on her chest. "Did you see what kind of car it was?"

Easton shook his head. "It was too dark. They tried to run me into a telephone pole."

"Thank goodness all officers go through defensive driving courses, or he might've plowed straight into that pole." Willow ran a hand over her arm in response to the chill that must've washed over her skin.

"And you want Willow to stay here because you think…" Lou didn't even know how to finish that thought.

Easton motioned to the dining room table. "That's a bit of a longer story."

"Anyone want tea?" Lou asked, moving to the kitchen to

turn on her hot water kettle as Willow and Easton sat. They both said they did, so Lou readied three mugs with herbal tea while the water heated.

"The attempt on my life tonight confirmed something I'd been thinking since we found Tyson in the barn last night." Easton sighed. "The fact that Tyson had that list of my schedule, at first, seemed like it could've been used to make sure I *wasn't* home when he came by to steal something. But it also could've been to figure out when I *would* be home, and the most vulnerable."

Lou tensed at the wording. She made sure her hands were steady before she poured the now boiling water into the mugs.

"After what happened tonight, I believe Tyson showing up at the house last night was actually supposed to be an attempt on my life."

"Like a hit?" Lou walked over, setting down the two mugs of tea in front of her friends before going back for her own and joining them at the table.

"Yes." Easton cleared his throat. "That's what bugged me most about the theory that he was there to steal something. Based on the schedule he'd made, I should've been home. I wasn't supposed to be working late last night. I stayed because we found out someone's been dumping hazardous waste on rural roads in the county, and I wanted to go over the reports before I headed home, but that was a last-minute decision. Tyson expected me to be there."

"And he knew Willow would be here," Lou whispered. They'd been doing their Tuesday night get-togethers for the past two months, finding it easiest to have a set day of the week to plan on spending time together instead of waiting for everyone's schedules to align. Sometimes Cricket could make it, other times it was just Willow, George, and Lou, but they had a standing time set aside each Tuesday evening.

The anger that tightened Easton's features answered any lingering questions in Lou's mind about why he and Willow were at her apartment.

"Chevelle Hayes, the boss of the Muscle Car Mafia is up for parole again next week. I blocked his first attempt two years ago, stating that he was far too dangerous to let out early, and that three years was nowhere near enough time for him to serve. I think he might be attempting to get me out of the way before he goes up against the parole board again."

"And he thinks that's not going to look suspicious?" Lou scoffed. "If the week before his parole hearing, the officer who put him in jail in the first place mysteriously dies?"

Lou immediately regretted using that final word, noting how Willow appeared close to tears at the thought.

Easton's shoulders lifted in a shrug. "It doesn't matter how it looks if he's careful enough. Even though we believe it's him, we don't have proof. My team searched through Tyson's apartment today, but found nothing in the way of communications between him and Hayes. They did find a letter with my address inside and an amount written next to it that would suggest a hit. There wasn't a return address on the letter, though, and it's unlikely Hayes sent it himself. But I wouldn't put it past him to have someone on the outside who does that for him."

Willow's expression only grew grimmer.

"And he's using his old crew to do the dirty work?" Lou asked.

Easton fiddled with the tea tag sticking out of his mug. "That's what we believe. The letter also said something about how it's no longer about a team. It's everyone for themselves this time."

"Then just bring in everyone who was on his crew," Lou said. "All six—er—five of them, now that Cobra's gone."

"That's the thing." Easton's tone dropped, along with his shoulders. "The only thing we've ever been able to figure out about his crew is their nicknames. We only got Chevelle because of a mistake, and when he talks about his crew, he uses their nicknames. He gives up trivial information that won't help us identify them, like their signature way to steal cars. It makes it seem like he's cooperating, but we know he's holding back their real identities. We only figured out Tyson was Cobra after he was dead."

Lou gulped. "So you have five people trying to kill you, and you have no idea who they are?"

CHAPTER 5

Easton swallowed before he said, "That's correct. Based on the letter we found at Cobra's apartment, I think Chevelle Hayes has put out a hit on me, and his crew are fighting for the chance to take me out so they can be the one to collect the money. That's my theory of how Cobra-slash-Tyson ended up dead in our barn. And it's why I need Willow to stay with you until I figure this out."

Lou told Willow she was welcome to stay as long as she needed to.

Willow pouted for a moment, reiterating that she wasn't happy about leaving her house. "But I understand Easton will think clearer if I'm out of harm's way," she added, as if the two of them had already had this same conversation in private.

"The chief's insisting on placing an officer outside the house during the evenings as well, just in case," Easton assured her.

"OC and Steve are going to go to the Milton farm for a brief vacation, starting tomorrow," Willow added, as if knowing Lou would worry about the animals as well. "Peggy Lee says she has an old paddock they can roam around in during the day, and Beau will put them in the barn at night. There are a few stalls inside."

While Peggy Lee Milton's farm was more about growing plants, Lou remembered seeing a small paddock and a field by the house. The two would be more than comfortable there, and would probably be spoiled beyond belief if Peggy Lee and Beau had their way. While Beau's size intimidated most people at first glance, animals weren't judgmental; the hulking young man preferred them because of this. He would take great care of Willow's animals.

With the explanations over, Easton and Willow said their goodbyes, and within minutes, Lou and Willow were working together to put clean sheets on the guest bed.

Lou studied her best friend as they secured the fitted sheet to the mattress. "Sorry, Willow. This is super stressful."

Willow closed her eyes in a long blink. "I'm worried about Easton. I know he can handle himself, but these are seasoned criminals."

"Criminals, yes. Killers? Not as much. Right? They're used to stealing cars, not taking out detectives. Maybe that will work in Easton's favor."

"True." Willow swallowed, opening her eyes and meeting Lou's with the most hopeful look she seemed to be able to muster.

"Did Easton tell you what their signature car-stealing methods were?" Lou asked, tucking in the flat sheet before turning to grab the comforter. "None of them were violent, right?"

Willow's mouth tensed as she recalled the information. "One of them was a grifter who used their good looks and charm to trick people into handing over their keys. Another hot-wired the cars. One was a skilled pickpocket, and they stole the keys without the victim noticing. One hacked into the computer systems of newer cars. They called one of them the infiltrator, because that person would worm into the inner circle of whoever they were stealing from and gain their trust, snatching the cars right out from under them the moment they let their guard down. And the last one would beat up their victims, taking the car once they were incapacitated." She pulled the comforter toward her as Lou tossed the pillows in place.

Lou had to concede that the last one didn't leave her feeling optimistic, but it wouldn't help Willow to dwell on that. "Right, so only one of them is known for using violence to get what they're after. I'd say those are great odds for Easton."

A small smile flickered across Willow's worried face. "True. Thanks, Lou. I hope you're right."

"Me too," Lou whispered, stopping at the door on her way out.

With that, she left Willow to get some sleep, but Lou had a feeling that sleep would be hard to come by for both of them.

THE NEXT MORNING, Willow left early to transport OC and Steve to their temporary lodgings at Milton Farm, and Lou spent a busy morning in the bookshop. The place was hopping. This being her third Valentine's Day at Whiskers and Words, the locals had come to anticipate Lou's love-themed book displays. Many stopped by to see what she'd done this year.

The retired community came in full force during the morning hours. There was a small lull during lunch. And then customers came in droves after getting off work or picking up their kids from school.

The locals absolutely loved Lou's displays. Seeing their joyful reactions and hearing the discussions surrounding them made all the effort worth it.

"I found one of my favorite reads of the year through that Blind Date with a Book table," she heard from multiple customers hanging around the brown-paper-covered books scattered on the back table.

They swarmed her Love to Hate It display, giggling at the critical reviews of popular books. Many of them picked up books because of the reviews, claiming to love something the reviewer hated. Other readers perused the recommendations of alternative titles to read if they disliked a popular book.

But the biggest hit, by far, was the puzzle display. Lou hadn't realized how starved for puzzles the people of Button were. The logic puzzle about the shop cats went quickly, and Lou had to print out a whole new stack of them. She also ordered more of the logic puzzle books since she sold out just before closing.

Willow returned as the sun was setting and Lou was locking up the bookshop for the day, but she didn't come alone. In the back of her truck were two very interesting-looking trees. They had long, yellow catkins hanging from the end of each branch.

"Those look like they could be from a Dr. Seuss book," Lou

said with a chuckle as she stepped out in front of the bookshop to help Willow.

"They're hazelnut trees. Aren't they cool?" Willow beamed. "To thank you for letting me stay here. Sorry, I've been a little behind with getting something for you to display here."

Lou scoffed, waving off her friend's worry. "You've been busy."

While Willow often brought over trees from the nursery to set in front of the shop, there hadn't been anything for the past month. She'd been too consumed with getting Easton moved in, renting out his house, and dealing with the almost constant needs of the new renters.

As if Lou mentioning how busy Willow had been lately had somehow reminded her tenants about the needy precedent they'd set, Willow's phone buzzed with an incoming text. Actually, from the back-to-back buzzing, the renters had sent a dozen texts all at once.

Willow groaned. "Sorry, I have to go," she said, her smile turning sour.

"More issues with the house?" Lou wiped the dirt off her hands.

Drawing in a thoughtful breath, Willow said, "I wish. No, now it's that they want to move out."

"Seriously? Can they even do that with the lease they signed?"

"They're trying to use the fact that there was a murder at our place to void the agreement since they no longer feel safe." Willow rolled her eyes. "I've got to go convince them that Easton has everything under control."

"Are you sure it wouldn't be for the better if they did move out?" Lou directed a worried glance at Willow.

But her friend ran a restless hand through her hair, finger-combing out a knot. "At first, I thought it might be. But Easton reminded me they were the most normal of all the people we interviewed. If they leave, we might get someone even worse in their place, and at least they keep everything nice and clean. We've heard horror stories about places that were destroyed by messy or careless renters on the forums we joined for tips about getting into the rental market." A shiver passed over her.

"Here. I'll come with you. Let me grab my purse."

If Willow was going anywhere near her house, Lou wasn't going to let her go alone. While the killers were after Easton, she wouldn't put it past them to hurt Willow to get to the detective.

They drove in silence out to Pattern Drive, all business as they parked at the house to the right, instead of Willow's on the left. As they made the trip up the walkway to the porch, Lou could see in more detail what Willow had been saying about the state they were keeping the house. Not only did the porch look just as clean—if not more—than when Easton occupied it, but the couple had included some outdoor furniture and plants to brighten up the space. It was a far cry from the detective's sparse style.

Willow rang the doorbell. Footsteps thumped on the hardwood floors as someone approached. When the door swung open, a woman in her late twenties or early thirties stood in the threshold.

"Hey, Rachel," Willow said, pulling out her phone and wiggling it in the air. "Got your messages."

Rachel Ashley's eyes narrowed ever so slightly as she clocked Lou's presence, but she quickly focused on Willow, saying, "Thanks for coming. Micah's in the dining room." She stepped back so they could enter.

Willow and Lou slipped off their shoes in the entryway before following Rachel to the large table next to the kitchen where a handsome man sat. He was trim in a way that reminded Lou of Ben, her late husband. Ben had always been in good shape because of his habit of running and wasn't one to put on a lot of bulky muscle. Ben had joked that he had little need for muscles in his job as an English professor, and they didn't help him in his other pastime of reading.

But this man's physique was the only thing he had in common with Lou's late husband. It wasn't even Micah's light blond hair that set him apart from Ben, whose hair had been almost black. The biggest difference was that while Ben exuded happiness, Micah Ashley was practically buzzing with pent-up anger.

"So, are you finally going to tell us what happened next door?" Micah asked as the three women sat down around the table. His question crackled through the room.

Lou didn't have to wonder which of the Ashleys was pushing the whole "move out" narrative. As if to punctuate that point, Rachel squirmed in her seat, glancing down at her lap.

Willow, to her credit, stayed calm. "I can't tell you everything, given that it's an ongoing investigation, but what I can say is that Easton and his officers have everything under control."

Pride flared in Lou's chest at her friend's composure. Willow had a tendency to be hotheaded, and Lou was surprised to see how well she contained her true feelings about the renters in the face of Micah's thinly veiled accusations, which made it sound as if Willow and Easton were purposefully keeping information from them.

"You'll excuse the question, Willow, but *what* exactly do they have under control?" Rachel spoke up, putting a hand on the table as if to signal to Micah that she was taking it from there. "We hear a bunch of racket on Tuesday night, then there are tons of cop cars. The officers took out what looked to be a body bag, and now there are cops stationed across the street at night, watching your house." The woman's hazel eyes were bright and sincere as they flicked from Willow to Lou and back again.

Exhaling in a huff, Willow said, "I understand. I really cannot tell you much. For your peace of mind, however, I can let you know that there was a man in the barn Tuesday night. He was dead when we arrived. We believe that he's part of a group that has a vendetta against Easton, and they're competing to see who can get to him first, which is why the security detail has been posted to watch the house. There's nothing to be worried about on your end. It's all directed at Easton."

"Unless we become collateral damage," Micah mumbled.

Rachel flared her eyes at him in warning. "Thank you for telling us that much. Is Easton okay?" The concern in her voice hit Lou straight in the chest, causing her throat to tighten with emotion.

It must've had the same effect on Willow because she swallowed, unable to speak at first. "They know a lot more now than they did on Tuesday. They'll figure this out."

"And they think that another one of the group members killed the man in the barn?" Rachel asked, confusion still marring her delicate features.

"It's a little difficult to understand, but yes. That's our best guess at this point." Willow offered them a smile, a big accomplishment considering how much Lou knew it pained her friend to think of people fighting over the chance to hurt Easton. Sighing, Willow added, "Look, I know that it's uncomfortable to think about a crime happening so close to home, but we really would appreciate it if you two would stay."

Rachel and Micah exchanged a long look, one that contained multiple unspoken conversations. Finally, they nodded.

"Okay, Willow. We won't move out, as long as this doesn't put my wife or myself in danger." Micah's blue eyes were sharp as they dug into Willow.

She stood. "I promise it won't."

Lou followed suit, giving Willow's tenants a tight nod as she did so. The two women turned toward the front door to leave, but they were stopped by a quiet sound from Rachel. When they turned back toward her, Rachel held up her index finger.

"Actually, Willow, before you go, would you mind checking the dishwasher for us?" Rachel's nose bunched up with discomfort. "It's making that sound again, and I swear I can hear water splashing underneath."

Willow's fingers curled tighter for just a moment, but she relaxed her hands and said, "Sure, I'll look at it right now."

CHAPTER 6

Whiskers and Words was quiet the following morning. Willow had gone to the nursery, and Lou's regulars were in attendance, though uncharacteristically silent.

All except George, that was.

"And then it hit me. I think the only reason I like Wesley is because I can't have him." George tapped her foot. "It's just like when I decided I needed a new gaming system just because it was sold out, and then when it finally became available again, I realized I didn't actually need anything new. So, anyway, that's why I'm glad I've decided to quash my feelings." George shrugged to punctuate her point. The indifferent gesture was completely at odds with the intense, emotional rambling that had preceded it for the past twenty minutes.

"That sounds like it's for the best," Lou told her friend. "I'm glad you feel good about the decision."

Her attention wandered over to the rest of her regulars. Forrest had his nose buried in a new science fiction book he'd purchased that morning, his fingers equally buried in Anne

Mice's dense gray fur as she snuggled in his lap. Silas held his newspaper high, almost as if he were hiding behind it. Catnip Everdeen wasn't in her usual place by his side, but that wasn't a surprise given George's rambling. As much as the orange-and-white cat loved Silas, she hated loud noises. Even if she had come out to see him at first, George's ranting had probably scared her back into one of her usual hiding places.

And Cricket sat at the table, her fingers kneading into her temple as she flipped through a quilting book. If Lou didn't know better, the pictures and patterns were giving her a headache. But Lou *did* know better. Especially since Cricket had continually shot exasperated glances at George while she'd been talking and looked like she might break into a round of applause now that George was done. Lou gave Cricket a warning scowl as the woman adjusted her seat. George needed to talk through her feelings.

Still, as much as Lou was happy to be there for George while she processed her emotions, she wasn't sad once the regulars slowly filed out and left her to the quiet of her bookshop.

All she wanted was a drama free rest of the day.

So, when Wesley St. James entered Whiskers and Words about an hour before closing that evening, Lou felt the surprise like a punch to the gut. She hadn't seen the private investigator since their previous case last fall.

Even more surprising was the cat carrier he held at his side.

The sight was so surprising that Lou dropped the new roll of tape she was trying to wrangle into the dispenser next to her register. The tape rolled under the counter, causing Lou to huff out a sigh and decide to grab it later.

"Wesley, hey." Lou stepped out from behind the counter as he approached.

"Hey, Lou." Wesley heaved the cat crate up onto the table, giving her a hint at how big the cat was before she even caught sight of his larger-than-normal frame. "Got a new foster for you, if you want him."

"He's huge." Lou peered through the bars of the carrier at a massive tomcat with brownish-black fur. "Sebastian didn't want him?"

One of Wesley's primary clients was the billionaire, Sebastian Andrade, who lived in a lavish house on the hill behind Button. The man had a soft spot for rescuing cats. In fact, he had more cats than even Lou at the moment.

"Well, I haven't actually asked him yet," Wesley admitted. "But that's because he's out of the country for the next two weeks, and I can't take the cat, so…"

"Oh. Uh, sure. He can stay here. Let's take him in the back and keep him separated from the others until I can have Noah examine him." She eyed the felines slowly creeping closer out of interest.

The black cat hissed as Wesley hefted the crate off the table. Lou couldn't be sure whether the hiss had been directed at Wesley or the other cats, which made her glad he would be quarantined from the others at first.

"Where'd you find him?" Lou asked.

Wesley coughed out a laugh. "Funny story. So, I've been doing a little … surveillance for a client in Kirk over the past week, and this guy keeps threatening to ruin my cover. Everywhere I try to hide in this particular business park, he finds me and starts making a racket, hissing and growling. Almost got me caught last night. So, I went out today with some food and used it to trick him into this crate. Now that he's off the streets, I might be able to do my job tonight."

Setting the crate on the floor, Wesley stepped back. Lou opened the metal door and then followed Wesley's lead. The black cat crept out of the crate, golden eyes flashing at the humans before he hissed and rushed into the corner of the room behind boxes of new inventory Lou had yet to put on the shelves.

Wesley tugged on his hair. "He's a little rough around the edges, but he'll probably be fine once he settles in." Then, as if Lou looked like she needed more convincing, he added, "If he's a pain, I can ask Sebastian to take him when he gets back from his trip."

"I'm sure he'll calm down once he settles in," Lou assured Wesley.

Making sure there were cozy bedding options as well as food, a litter box, and water for the new cat, Lou and Wesley exited the office, closing the door behind them.

Wesley slipped his hands in his coat pockets.

"Hey, do you know anything about the Muscle Car Mafia?" Lou asked before Wesley could leave.

Frowning, Wesley said, "Never heard of it. Is it, like, a driving video game or something?" His frown deepened as he realized who he was talking to, and that Lou wasn't the sort to play video games.

She shook her head. "They're real, and local. Apparently, they used to steal cars in the area, about five to seven years ago." She stopped, unsure how much Easton wanted out in the community. But Wesley was a private investigator, and there wasn't anyone else in the shop. "This stays between you and me, but…" She leaned closer and told him about the attempts on Easton's life and the reasoning behind it.

Wesley's blue eyes grew bigger as her story progressed. By the end, he was running his fingers through his floppy blond hair. "Actually, I think I might know someone who had a car stolen … or almost stolen? One of my clients, Doug Cromwell. He's a big car collector, and I remember him saying something about an attempted theft about five years ago. I don't know if it was the same group, but it sounds like the right time period."

It sounded like a lot of people had cars stolen in the area around that time, so Lou wasn't sure how that would help her. "Okay, well, if you hear anything about the Muscle Car Mafia from any of your sources, would you let me know?"

"Absolutely." He gave a clipped nod toward the door, checking his watch. "I've gotta head out now, but thanks for taking the cat, Lou."

She waved goodbye to Wesley and brought out her phone to text Noah.

> Hey, you. New cat came in today. Do you have time tonight to look at him?

She sent the message and then ducked behind the register to grab the roll of tape she'd dropped when Wesley had arrived.

The bell on the front door dinged.

"I do," Noah said as he strode into the bookshop, tucking his phone into his pocket.

Lou popped up, the tape in hand. "Oh, hi. What a nice surprise."

"My last surgery of the day canceled. Came to see what

you were up to." He closed the distance between them, wrapping his arms around her as he kissed her in greeting. "So, a new cat?"

"He's in the back. I'll take you to see him." Lou moved to the front door to lock it and change the sign. It was only ten minutes until closing, so it wouldn't be a huge deal to close a little early. "Wesley just brought him in."

Noah's eyebrows shot up. "Wesley? We haven't heard from him in a while."

"From? No. About? All morning." Lou groaned as she filled Noah in on George's rant that morning about the guy and her feelings for him.

"Sounds like she's gotten over her fear of talking about him around anyone but you." Noah's brown eyes danced with humor.

"Quite quickly," Lou agreed. "She was worried about telling Willow on Tuesday, and now all the regulars know. And they didn't even seem excited to learn about the news. Usually that lot is as eager as they come to hear about new or forbidden romances blooming in town. But today, they went straight from ignorant to annoyed." She giggled.

Noah's lips pulled into a soft smile. "George has always been a verbal processor. It's nice of you to be there to listen while she figures everything out."

Lou inclined her head as they entered the office. A black blur streaked across the room, hissing as it went. "He's a little shy."

Noah immediately switched into veterinarian mode. It took them a few tries to catch him. The cat not only tried to scratch and bite Noah, but he turned out to be a master of slipping out of their grip despite how big he was.

With the help of an old towel that Lou kept around for just such an occasion, Noah was able to do a preliminary exam on the cat.

"He's got fleas, which we can take care of. He's a little dehydrated, which you've already seen to." Noah pointed at the fresh water and food Lou had set up for him in the office. "And he's also got a bad attitude." As if to prove him right, the cat let out a low growl. Noah placed the flea treatment on his neck and set him on the floor. "But other than that, he's healthy."

Lou's chest felt tight as the cat skittered back into the corner. "We'll just have to show him that he's safe. Do you want to stay for dinner?"

"I'd love to."

They left the cat in the office, heading upstairs. They were just sitting down to dinner when Willow clomped into the apartment. Her cheek was streaked with mud, and there was a twig in her brown hair.

"Everything okay?" Lou asked, jumping up to take Willow's bag as she sagged in the doorway.

"Yeah, just a long day of moving plants and stacking bags of compost and mulch. It doesn't help that I haven't been able to sleep for more than an hour at a time since Tuesday." Willow slumped against the wall.

Lou wrapped her arm through Willow's, guiding her over to the table. "Here, have some food, and then you can go to bed early. Noah and I made … soup?" She wasn't sure what to call the stew-like bean-and-vegetable dish they were dipping crusty bread into, but it was hearty, cozy, and likely just what Willow needed at the end of a long day.

"Any news from Easton?" Noah asked once they were all seated around the table and eating once more.

"Nothing new," Willow said. "They can't prove Chevelle Hayes is the one who put out the hit. There's not much more out there to warn Easton about who the members of the crew are, and who might come for him. Basically, he just has to keep his head on a swivel until next Friday when the parole hearing happens."

Lou and Noah tried to cheer her up, but once Willow finished her meal, she disappeared into the spare bedroom, saying something about needing a shower.

"I'm worried about her. She's exhausted," Lou whispered.

"I don't blame her. If someone was threatening you, Marigold, or my family, I wouldn't be able to sleep either."

Lou chewed on her lip for a moment before turning back to her meal, finishing the last bite. Noah grabbed their dishes, and as he cleaned up, Lou leaned on the counter and contemplated what she could do to help her friend.

CHAPTER 7

Lou and Noah settled on the couch after cleaning the kitchen. Instead of turning on the television, which might've been too loud for Willow to fall asleep to, they opted for light piano music and conversation. If Willow had any chance of catching up on sleep, Lou would gladly help.

Soon the sound of steady breathing spilled out from under the door of the spare bedroom, and Lou felt some of the weight lift off her shoulders. But Willow getting much needed rest was only part of the issue at hand.

Noah understood just what Lou was thinking, as usual, because he launched into talk of the problems they faced. "So, Easton's the target of a hit. They're pretty sure they know who hired the hit, but can't prove it. They know the members of Chevelle's old crew are the ones who will likely take the job, but only know them by nicknames," Noah summarized, his voice a whisper as they scooted closer together on the couch.

As much as Lou was tempted to say they could leave and go to his place so they wouldn't have to tiptoe around, she didn't want to leave Willow alone, given the circumstances. Plus, she didn't mind an excuse to get close to Noah.

Glancing over at her coffee table, Lou grabbed at the notepad sitting haphazardly on a stack of books. "There has to be something we're not seeing." She clicked on her pen and wrote out what Noah had just listed.

> Chevelle Hayes wants Easton out of the way since Easton blocked his last attempt at parole, and he has another hearing next week.

> Chevelle Hayes is the leader of a group called the Muscle Car Mafia. It is made up of seven members, including him. These members were nick-named after different muscle cars. We don't know their real names.

Checking with Noah, Lou waited for him to signal that they were on the same page.

"We know the real name for one of them," Noah said, tapping the page.

"Right." Lou added another note.

> Tyson Krate was Cobra. He was killed with a knife to the chest during an attempt to kill Easton at the house on Tuesday, proving there must be a substantial award for the hit, and the others are competing to get the money.

Lou tapped the pen against her lip as she thought. "Oh, we also know that each of the members of the group had a unique way of stealing cars. Willow was telling me this the other night."

Noah listened as Lou wrote that information as well. She snorted at the list. "This almost looks like the clues for a logic puzzle." Her laugh stopped short, caught in her throat. "Wait. I wonder…" She flipped to a blank page and started tracing out a grid, just like she had when she'd made the puzzle about the cats in the shop, their fur color, and their favorite places to sleep.

"You think this might work?" Noah peered over Lou's shoulder as she made sure there were six columns and six rows in each of the three sections.

Lou didn't stop her line work. "It can't hurt. There are six members of the Muscle Car Mafia with six nicknames, six different actual identities, and six unique ways to steal cars." She filled in the information, narrating as she went. "There was Cobra, Mustang, GTO, Viper, Firebird, and Daytona. Their methods for stealing were pickpocketing, hot-wiring, computer hacking, infiltration, charm, and violence." Lou jotted them down. "As for their real names, we only know one of those." Lou wrote Tyson Krate on the first line in the third section. "But we do know that he was Cobra."

She placed an O in the box where Tyson and Cobra met on the matrix, then put Xs along each row and column to show that no one else in the crew was known by that nickname.

	Cobra	Mustang	Daytona	Viper	GTO	Firebird	Hotwire	Hack	Charm	Infiltrate	Violence	Pickpocket
Tyson Krate	O	X	X	X	X	X						
	X											
	X											
	X											
	X											
	X											
Hotwire												
Hack												
Charm												
Infiltrate												
Violence												
Pickpocket												

"But Tyson/Cobra's dead, and we don't have any information on how he liked to steal cars." Noah studied the puzzle in front of them.

Lou inhaled. "Oh, actually I might know. Willow mentioned that Tyson had a record. He was arrested when he was younger, for petty theft. I'd bet anything that he's our pickpocket." She filled in the corresponding box, adding the Xs to block that style of stealing out from the other members of the team.

	Cobra	Mustang	Daytona	Viper	GTO	Firebird	Hotwire	Hack	Charm	Infiltrate	Violence	Pickpocket
Tyson Krate	O	X	X	X	X	X	X	X	X	X	X	O
	X											X
	X											X
	X											X
	X											X
	X											X
Hotwire	X											
Hack	X											
Charm	X											
Infiltrate	X											
Violence	X											
Pickpocket	O	X	X	X	X	X						

But as far as it felt like those clues had gotten them, they immediately hit a dead end. As far as information went, that was it. Until they knew more about the group, or who might be part of it, they were at a standstill with their puzzle, and with this investigation.

THE NEXT MORNING, Lou brought the puzzle downstairs with her as she opened the bookshop. She'd added one clue to the area beneath the puzzle.

Tyson Krate had a cobra tattoo on his forearm, and he was arrested for pickpocketing when he was a teenager.

She couldn't think of anything else to add by the time her regulars began pouring in, shivering against the frigid February temperatures. Lou took that as a hint to start a fire. Once she was done, her four regulars were seated in the middle of the shop, surrounded by cats.

"Hey, while I have the group of you here…" Lou raised an eyebrow as she got an idea. Seeing they were waiting to be filled in on what she was thinking, Lou said, "I have a new cat. He's pretty scared, and I'm wondering whether he'll do better once he's introduced to the other cats."

The new cat had still been upset and wary when she'd checked on him before Noah had gone home last night. He'd seemed no more confident or comfortable in his environment after being there for hours. In fact, he almost appeared angrier, which told Lou she needed to try something different.

"Sure. We can help." George placed her hands on her knees as if she might stand. She'd come alone that morning, citing that Geralt had looked too comfortable, and she hadn't wanted to move him. "What can we do?"

Lou swallowed, thinking through the logistics of her plan. "I think he'll be fine around the other cats, but just in case he gets aggressive, would you guys scoop them up and get them out of his way?"

They each nodded, assigning themselves to a cat. Silas was going to watch out for Catnip. Forrest would make sure Anne was safe. George was on Meatball duty, and Cricket was watching Charles Lickens. Lou knew Sapphire was the safest, asleep up on the table, but she would be his shadow once she freed the new cat.

Confident that the place was as set up for him as it was going to get, Lou opened the office door. She snuck around the corner, waiting. After a few moments, the black cat poked his head out the doorway and slunk from the office into the main bookstore.

He was crouched low, like Catnip often moved when she was feeling scared or insecure. It quickly became apparent that it wasn't the cats who had him upset, but the people. In fact, he didn't pay the cats any attention, not even when Charles came right up to sniff him. No, the black cat merely walked past the British Blue, his focus fixed on Cricket. The older woman backed up.

"Watch it there, buddy." She held her foot forward, as if she might be able to scoot him back if he got too close.

A low growl started in the cat's throat, and he glowered at Cricket. He moved on after a few seconds, but not without studying her with an intensity that felt like a warning. He wended his way through the shop just like that, growling and hissing at each of the humans, ignoring the other cats.

"Odd." George snorted. "He sure is angry."

The cat finally settled in front of the fireplace, tucking his legs under him until he was in a loaf shape.

"Looks like a simple case of a bad cat to me," Silas said, sniffing as he turned back to his newspaper. Catnip had remained by his side, ironically not scared of this angry new feline, even though she was terrified of everything else in the world.

"He's not a bad cat." Lou crossed her arms. "He's just …
misunderstood."

"So you're keeping him?" Cricket asked, the question
shooting out of her like water spilling through a pressurized
dam.

Lou gestured to where he was lying in front of the fireplace. "He seems fine now that he's warm. Maybe he got too
cold in the office." She walked toward him, her hand held out
slightly.

But the moment he noticed her coming his way, his head
whipped toward her, and he growled.

"Well, I take that back. Maybe he needs a little more time."

"Louisa Henry, you cannot have a mean cat like that loose
in a store where you have customers." Cricket crossed her
arms.

"She's right, Lou." Forrest's tone was low and serious.
"Remember the issue you had that one time Sapphire clawed a
customer? This would be ten times worse."

Lou's chest tightened at the memory, at the fear she'd felt
after it had happened. Sapphire had been startled. The woman
had come over to him and pet him roughly without giving him
a warning that she was there. This wasn't a case of a deaf cat
being surprised. Forrest was right. This new cat had obvious
issues with people and, based on what Wesley had told her,
and what the cat had just done to Cricket, he might hunt her
customers if he was given free rein of the bookshop. He wasn't
ready for that just yet.

"Yeah, I agree." Lou let out a defeated sigh. "Okay, come on
NF. You've gotta hang out in the office a little while longer,
until I can figure out what to do with you." Lou stepped closer
to the cat, ignoring its hisses and growls.

Once she was within a few feet, the cat got up and skittered away from her. She kept following it until it slunk back into the office and she shut the door.

"NF? Is that what you called it?" George squinted one eye. "What does that stand for?"

Lou's expression softened. "Oh, well, I don't want to come up with a name for him yet since I'm sure we don't really understand his personality yet." She cut a decisive look at Silas. "So I figured I'd call him NF until I do. I was thinking it could stand for New Foster. But it could also be New Friend, or even New Feline."

"More like BF for Bad Feline," Silas muttered.

Hand on her hip, Lou said, "We don't know that yet, Silas. We should give him the benefit of the doubt until we get to know him better."

"Yeah, sure. Benefit of the doubt. Just ask the long list of victims I'm sure he's attacked if they wish they'd given him the benefit of the doubt. They'd know better than anyone what we're dealing with."

Despite his discouraging statement, Lou's mind clicked with a new thought at his wording. Victims. She might've been at a standstill with information from Chevelle about his Muscle Car Mafia, but the other people who might give her information on the group and its members were the victims, the people who had cars stolen during the crew's reign of terror in the region.

"Why do you look like a light bulb just went on over your head?" Cricket asked with a snort of laughter.

Lou explained her revelation.

"You're welcome." Silas removed his signature bowler hat for a moment, tipping it toward her.

"But do we know any victims?" George asked, appraising the group.

"Wesley does," Lou answered before she fully realized her mistake.

"Wesley?" George coughed.

Silas puffed out his cheeks. "Here we go."

Heat crept up Lou's neck and into her jawline. "Uh, yeah. He was here yesterday, bringing in NF." Lou pointed to the office where the cat was, not because she thought George might've forgotten which cat she was talking about but because she hoped George might direct her glower of hatred elsewhere for even a second; it was that piercing. "While he was here, Wesley mentioned he might know someone who had a car stolen around the same time the MCM was operating."

"Wesley brought in that cat?" George spat out the question, ignoring the rest of the information. "Why would he bring it to you?"

Lou's shoulders bumped up in a shrug, feigning nonchalance. "Sebastian's out of the country, and Wesley said he doesn't want a cat, so he brought him here."

It didn't sound that wild to Lou, given the fact people brought her cats all the time, but somehow her explanation made George even more upset.

"He said he doesn't want a cat? That's rich." She began pacing. "Of course he'd hate cats. He knows how much Geralt means to me." Whirling back to Lou, George said, "See? This is just another reason we wouldn't be good for one another." Laughing in a way that was a bit unhinged, George stomped toward the door, yelled something about getting ready for a competition with her D and D group, then stormed out of the shop, leaving the rest of them in stunned silence.

"Okaaay." Cricket's eyes were wide. She turned back to Lou. "So Wesley knew someone who had cars stolen by the MCM?"

"It wasn't Sebastian, was it?" Forrest asked Lou.

"No. Doug Cromwell. Do you know him?"

"Only *of* him," Cricket scoffed.

"And his money," Silas added.

Forrest cleared his throat, as if embarrassed by their lack of tact. "He lives on a rather large piece of land close to Sebastian's house, actually. Definitely keeps to himself. And, yes, the man is rather well-off."

"I suppose that makes sense if he's a big car collector," Lou mused.

"Does anyone know of someone locally who had a car stolen?" Lou asked. "I feel like talking to them might be our best bet for finding information about who was part of the Muscle Car Mafia. Right now, we've only got what we know about the dead guy, so anything helps."

Forrest glanced up at the ceiling. "I think one of my patients might've had a car stolen during that time period, but don't quote me on that. I'll ask around and find out."

"We all will," Cricket said, standing and moving to grab her jacket.

"Thanks," Lou said as they filed out together.

Once she was alone, she said, "And in the meantime, I'll pay Doug Cromwell a visit."

CHAPTER 8

Lou sent a text to Wesley that afternoon, asking if he could set up a meeting between her and Doug Cromwell about his car. When the private investigator answered back, letting her know Doug would be more than happy to talk with her over dinner that evening, Lou was ecstatic.

Given what she'd learned about the man's wealth from her regulars, she expected to receive a message with an address to an ornate mansion, as had been the case when she'd met both Sebastian Andrade and Francis Knight.

But the place she pulled up to was a roadside diner about halfway between Button and the Milton farm. In fact, it was buried so deep along an old, forgotten highway that Lou was sure the only way anyone would know it was there was by word of mouth.

The building wasn't anything special, and Lou wondered if she might be in the wrong place. After triple-checking the address, Lou caught sight of Wesley's Honda parked next to a very sleek, black car. She didn't even recognize the badge on the hood of the black car, proving it wasn't one of the standard brands. That definitely looked like the vehicle a rich car enthusiast might drive, even if this choice of restaurant didn't mesh with what she'd come to expect from other people of great fortune in the area.

Stepping forward, Lou felt a pull to the restaurant tucked into the base of a tree-lined hill. She wasn't sure if it was because the diner was the only sign of life in the middle of the mountainous back road, but it drew her in. The golden light spilling from its many windows, and the happy chatter she could hear from the parking lot, made her feel welcome.

Lou's guess about only locals knowing about the joint turned out to be truer than she first realized. Every head turned toward her when she stepped foot inside. It was a dead giveaway that they were used to recognizing anyone who walked through the door.

The interior of the place was decorated like a standard '50s diner, but the owners had leaned into the car theme. Booths made to look like the front or back end of classic cars were interspersed throughout the space. Bumpers, license plates, and even a whole side of a car stuck out from the walls next to old gas filling stations.

A hand raised above the booths of people staring at her, and Lou found Wesley sitting toward the back. She maneuvered her way through the tables, turning sideways a few times to get through more cramped areas. The servers must be very talented to navigate the place with trays of food and drink, she thought as she finally reached the table where Wesley sat.

"Lou, hey!" Wesley stood to greet her, motioning for her to take a seat in the booth next to him. As she scooted in, she found a man in his sixties seated across from them. "This is Doug Cromwell. Doug, this is Louisa Henry, the bookshop owner and local sleuth I was telling you about."

Doug dressed like he was trying to be Jay Leno. He wore a jean jacket that matched his jean pants, and he had a veritable pompadour of white hair. But whereas Jay Leno had that famously big chin, Doug resembled more of a turtle, without much of a jawline to speak of.

He nodded, making his chin disappear even farther into his neck. "Ah, yes. The woman who thinks she can solve the unsolvable puzzle of the Muscle Car Mafia." He didn't say the words in a mocking tone. On the contrary, his eyes shone with the prospect.

It was possible Wesley had oversold her qualifications to this poor man.

"I'm certainly going to try," Lou said. "Especially if it means that my friends can live without fear."

Doug turned his attention to his left as a server came over. "Tina, can we get a basket of fries, an order of waffles, fried chicken, and a round of Cokes for the table?"

Tina wore an old diner uniform. She'd curled and styled her hair like she was from the movie *Grease*. Honestly, the only thing missing was a pair of roller skates. She jotted down the order without even regarding Lou. "I'll have that right out, Dougie," she said in a voice that felt all too quiet for such a boisterous and crowded space.

Bristling at having this man she just met assume he would know what to order for her, Lou was about to say something when Wesley kicked her under the table. He kept his gaze forward, but she got the distinct impression that she shouldn't question the man's behavior.

Lou let her frustration surrounding the food order go and focused on the task ahead of her.

"So, Doug, Wesley tells me you might've had a car stolen by this group." She fixed him with a questioning stare.

"Not just any car. *The* car," Doug sputtered, obviously surprised she didn't know.

Lou expected him to start in on a long diatribe about why the car he owned was so special. She waited for words like rare and one-of-a-kind to come spilling out of his mouth, pride seeping through his tone as he described why everyone else was jealous enough of the car to try to steal it from him.

But instead of all that, Doug said, "It was during the job to steal my car that the police finally caught Chevelle."

Leaning forward with interest, Lou asked, "Really?"

Doug's eyes danced with a light that told Lou this was not the first, nor would it be the last, time that he told this story. In fact, Doug appeared to love telling it. He dove right in, each sentence obviously edited and revised over time to garner the most intrigue.

"It was a Friday night about five years back. I was supposed to be out of town, but I'd come down with a cold and stayed home. I'd already given my staff the time off, and I didn't want to call them back, especially since all I wanted to do was hole up for the weekend. I hunkered down with a vat of soup, intending to watch through the entire catalog of *Fast and Furious* movies." Doug smirked as if this was an accomplishment to be proud of, even though Lou found it a little overwhelming to consider. "It was during the end of the first movie that I heard the noise: the unmistakable rumble of my 1970 Plymouth 'Cuda."

As Doug talked, Tina delivered food and drinks to the

table. Lou was so engrossed in Doug's story that she barely noticed, though Wesley reached into the basket of fries and began munching on a few.

"Luckily, while I'd dismissed much of my house staff for the weekend, I had doubled up on security while I was set to be away. I'd been in such a cold-medicine-induced fog that I forgot to send the extra security home. The moment I heard that engine, I pressed the silent alarm, and the guards closed in. They didn't catch the second person, but Chevelle was mine—well, the police's." He sat back proudly, grabbing his drink and sucking a long sip of soda through the straw.

Lou digested the information. "And you have no idea what happened to the other person who was with him? The one that got away? Did your security guards notice anything about them?"

Doug grew excited by her question, and breathed in quickly, forgetting that he was still drinking the soda. He coughed and leaned forward until he could speak again. "Her, actually. And, yes, we found her. The police didn't quite believe me, but it doesn't matter anyway."

"Why's that?" Lou narrowed her eyes at him.

"By the time I had my private investigator, at the time, look into her, all he could find was a death certificate." Doug glanced at Wesley as if there might be a story behind why he now used Wesley instead of this other PI.

But Lou couldn't focus on that. "Dead?" Thoughts spun through Lou, making the loud, enclosed space feel like it was closing in on her. She met Doug's eyes. "Do you remember her name? What was it about her that made you certain she was the person with Chevelle that night?"

"Her name was Bex Mason. All the signs were there. She'd

grown up in her father's garage just north of Seattle. She was a master mechanic and knew how to hot-wire anything. She'd also recently come into money that her family couldn't explain, and would disappear on random nights throughout the week without notice. She lived alone, but her family noticed. They were worried. She was unaccounted for the night the police caught Chevelle, and her family said she was paranoid and jumpy after that. Until someone strangled her in her home about a month later. She also had a mustang tattoo, and everyone in that gang has a tattoo connected to their nickname, or so I'm told."

That got Lou's attention. It definitely tracked with the snake tattoo she'd seen on Cobra, which meant that Bex Mason might've been Mustang. "And why didn't the police believe you?" she asked.

"They're not exactly the biggest fans of private investigators," Wesley spoke up, answering that question.

Doug agreed. "And they argued that a lot of people have horse tattoos. But I could've sworn she had the same long, dark hair I saw sticking out from under that mask when I looked back on the security footage."

Even though the aroma of the fries, chicken, and waffles was mouthwatering, the information settled like a lead weight at the bottom of Lou's stomach, and she didn't think she'd be able to eat a thing. Instead, she pulled out her logic puzzle and filled in the second legal name: Bex Mason. Then she shaded in the boxes for Mustang and hot-wire, X-ing out the possibility for anyone else.

	Cobra	Mustang	Daytona	Viper	GTO	Firebird	Hotwire	Hack	Charm	Infiltrate	Violence	Pickpocket
Tyson Krate	O	X	X	X	X	X	X	X	X	X	X	O
Bex Mason	X	O	X	X	X	X	O	X	X	X	X	X
	X	X					X					X
	X	X					X					X
	X	X					X					X
	X	X					X					X
Hotwire	X	O	X	X	X	X						
Hack	X	X										
Charm	X	X										
Infiltrate	X	X										
Violence	X	X										
Pickpocket	O	X	X	X	X	X						

"Looks like you've got a good start there," Doug said, obviously being generous with his definition of a 'good start' in an attempt to cheer her up.

"Sure, but the only information we get is after one of the crew is killed, taken out by one of the other members of this group they were part of." Lou shivered.

"I thought I heard another member of the group had been apprehended about a year ago. That one's not dead, at least."

"Really?" Lou leaned forward. For the first time all evening, hope bloomed inside her chest.

CHAPTER 9

By the time Lou returned home from her meeting with Doug and Wesley, Willow was just sitting down at the table with a bowl of cereal. Lou held out the to-go container of french fries, fried chicken, and waffles Doug insisted she take.

"Want to add a confusing mix of diner food to that sad dinner of yours?" she asked.

Willow chuckled, but her eyes sparked at the sight of the containers. "I never say no to free food."

The cereal was quickly pushed aside as Willow started in on a waffle, groaning in appreciation. "This is so good. Thank you. Where'd you get it?" Willow asked in between bites.

"It was this funky diner out off the old highway. I went to talk to one of the victims of the Muscle Car Mafia. Wesley knows him. The guy goes there at least once a week and ordered for the table, then made me take the leftovers since no one ate more than a few bites."

"I've never even heard of the place." Willow giggled at the

absurdity, but her eyes locked on to Lou. "You're researching into the case?"

Lou took a beat to answer. "If I was, would that be okay?" She didn't want to go against Easton's orders, but she couldn't help worrying about her friends.

"*Okay?*" Willow scoffed. "I'd love it if you were on the case. Not that I think Easton and the officers can't handle it," she added quickly. "It's just that I worry about him, and who wouldn't want you in their corner? Did you learn anything?"

Lou relaxed now that she had Willow's approval. She grabbed the logic puzzle from her purse and laid it out on the table in between them. "It was Doug's house where Chevelle was finally caught."

"When did you make this?"

"Last night. Noah and I were talking through the clues, and we realized how close to a logic puzzle this sounded. The only problem is that we don't know most of the real identities of the group, so I went to Doug to see if he could give me any information on who tried to steal from him. Five years ago, he was supposed to be gone for the weekend, but got sick and stayed home instead, so he caught the whole thing. He said there was a second person with Chevelle that night, one who tried to hot-wire his classic Plymouth 'Cuda. They didn't count on him bumping up security. She got away, but Doug is convinced that Chevelle had her killed for the mistake."

"Easton didn't say anything about that." Willow's eyebrows rose higher on her forehead.

"Doug said the police didn't believe him. Well, actually, they said the evidence wasn't definitive. But it sounds promising."

Lou went over everything Doug's previous PI had found

and how he'd determined Bex Mason was Mustang from the Muscle Car Mafia.

Willow considered the evidence. "Sounds clear to me. It also doesn't surprise me that the police weren't willing to commit to that identification. They probably didn't want to upset her family unless they were positive."

"I understand." Lou eyed her friend. "But Doug also mentioned that another one of the Muscle Car Mafia members is in prison, serving time. Easton hasn't said anything about that?"

"Not a thing. Doug was sure?"

"As sure as he was about the identity of Mustang, and that she was killed for her mistake." Lou swallowed. "Is Easton working late tonight?"

"Yeah. I think he's been staying away from the house as much as he can. Honestly, I don't blame him. It's weird without Steve and OC there. Plus, the more time he's home, the more likely the Ashleys are to call him over to fix something." Willow took out her phone. "Let me see if he can stop by." She typed out a message and set her phone on the table once it was sent.

While they waited for his response, Willow grabbed a few of the fries from the container open in between them. Lou picked up a few more, finally feeling like she might have an appetite now that things were looking up in this case.

"Hey, what's with the cranky black cat locked in the office downstairs?" Willow asked after swallowing a bite.

"Oh, I forgot to tell you about him."

She filled her friend in on NF—or as Silas was calling him, BF—and how Wesley had brought him in. At the end of that explanation, Lou told Willow the drama that bringing up Wesley had caused with George.

"Yeah, sounds like she's definitely over him," Willow said facetiously.

About to answer, Lou was cut off by Willow's phone buzzing with an incoming message. "Easton says he's at the back door. I'll go let him in."

Lou stayed put, knowing the couple might need some time alone to greet one another. As she guessed, they were as close as could be as they emerged from the stairs and walked into the apartment. Easton had his arm around Willow's shoulder, and he was whispering something into her hair. Willow's arms were clasped around Easton's waist, and she laughed at whatever he said.

Upon seeing Lou, Easton straightened and cleared his throat. "Sorry, Lou. I just really missed this one."

Lou's heart warmed at the sight. "Never apologize for that. I'm sorry you two have to be apart."

"Even more so because we were just getting used to living together, only to have it ripped away like this." Easton looked tired, and Lou wondered if he was finding it just as hard to sleep without Willow as she was without him.

"That's kind of what we wanted to talk to you about," Willow said warily.

Easton eyed her and then Lou.

"Have a seat." Lou gestured to the to-go containers. "Help yourself to leftovers if you'd like."

The spark in Easton's gaze at the mention of food rivaled that of Willow's when she'd seen the same containers. He sat and plucked a few fries from the container while Willow put a waffle on a plate for him.

"Is this from that place out on the old highway?" Easton asked after swallowing his second bite.

"Yes, I met Doug Cromwell there tonight," Lou said.

Easton's knife slowed, then came to a stop in the middle of cutting off another bite of waffle. His attention cut to Willow, who smiled brightly at him.

"Lou noticed that the clues we have about the Muscle Car Mafia are a lot like a logic puzzle, and she was just trying to go to the source to find out if he had any more information," Willow explained.

"Which he did," Lou added, studying Easton carefully.

Easton dragged a breath through his nose. He sat back. "He told you he thinks Bex Mason was the second person at his house that night and that she's Mustang from the Muscle Car Mafia?"

"You don't?" Lou picked up another fry and popped it into her mouth.

"There are things that match up," Easton begrudgingly admitted. "But it's a lot easier for a private investigator to make a statement like that than it is for us. We need more proof."

"He also told me that another member of the group is already in prison."

Easton's jaw ticked at that.

"Wait. There is?" Willow asked, obviously reading that motion as an admission of guilt. "Why didn't you tell me?"

"Because," Easton said, his tone even but sharp, "I didn't think the two of you were getting involved, so why would you need to know any of this?" His shoulders sagged forward in defeat. "Plus, the guy's been in for over a year, and he's even more closed off than Chevelle when it comes to talking about the group. He's in for assault, and is a pretty terrifying guy. Believe me, we've already tried everything we can think of, but he won't say a word."

Lou and Willow shared a disappointed scowl, but they couldn't argue with that.

"Do you know who he is in this puzzle, though?" Lou tapped the paper in the middle of the table. "At least we could use the information to rule out other people from the group."

Easton hesitated, as if he was considering not telling her, but then he said, "His name is Fitz Grimes, but everyone calls him GTO."

"And if he's in for assault, it's probably safe to say that he's the one who used violence to procure the cars he stole?" Lou asked as she filled in the information on the puzzle.

Easton coughed. "Definitely. Brute force is his only quality."

	Cobra	Mustang	Daytona	Viper	GTO	Firebird	Hotwire	Hack	Charm	Infiltrate	Violence	Pickpocket
Tyson Krate	O	X	X	X	X	X	X	X	X	X	X	O
Bex Mason	X	O	X	X	X	X	O	X	X	X	X	X
Fitz Grimes	X	X	X	X	O	X	X	X	X	X	O	X
	X	X			X		X				X	X
	X	X			X		X				X	X
	X	X			X		X				X	X
Hotwire	X	O	X	X	X	X						
Hack	X	X			X							
Charm	X	X			X							
Infiltrate	X	X			X							
Violence	X	X	X	X	O	X						
Pickpocket	O	X	X	X	X	X						

Once the rest of the columns and rows were crossed out, Lou tapped her pen on the table. "Easton, you wouldn't mind if I tried to talk to him, would you?"

Easton scratched at his chin.

When he didn't answer right away, she added, "He might not talk to you because you're a cop. What if I can get something out of him because I'm not in law enforcement?"

"It's worth a try," Willow said.

The detective shifted in discomfort. "He's unhinged, Lou. He's not in the maximum security prison since the thing we brought him in for was beating up a few guys when a grand theft auto went sideways about a year back. But, if you ask me, the two were lucky to walk away with only a few broken ribs and black eyes. Based on the state we found a lot of his victims in, from his Muscle Car Mafia days, he's capable of a lot worse. We just didn't have the proof to link him to those other assaults, so we took what we could get."

The thought chilled Lou to her bones, but she had to try. "I'll be there during visiting hours, with guards watching. I'll be careful." Lou assured him.

"And I'll be there with her." Willow sat up straighter.

Easton hesitated, but knew he was already riding a fine line by keeping Willow out of their house. Dipping his head, he said, "Okay, see if you can find out anything from him."

CHAPTER 10

The contrast in Lou's day that Saturday was stark. She spent the morning in her cozy bookshop, decorated with pink and red hearts for Valentine's Day. At lunch, she closed the shop and picked up Willow from the nursery to go visit the local prison.

The cold concrete building didn't hold an ounce of holiday flair. It wasn't as if Lou expected a prison to be decorated at all, let alone for a holiday celebrating love, but it made the disparity all the more intense.

She and Willow checked in and were shown to a room with tables set up for visiting hours. The guards walked them through the rules and explained what to do if something went wrong or if there was an alarm during their visit. Lou gulped at the prospect, but took a seat next to Willow as they waited for Fitz Grimes to come through—*if* he would even see them, she reminded herself. Both Easton and the guards had mentioned that he might not want to speak to visitors, and they would have to respect his choice.

Lou's knee bounced. Her fingers ran along the edges of the

folded logic puzzle in her purse, needing the constant reassurance it was there. In her absolute best-case scenario, Fitz would at least confirm that the details she had up to that point were correct. As confident as she felt about the information she'd filled out so far, it was technically still nothing more than speculation.

During the past week, as she'd gotten into more difficult logic puzzles, there had been a few she'd hit dead ends on and had to start from scratch because she'd marked something she assumed instead of following exactly what was in the clues. Worry sat in her stomach at the thought that she might be doing the same thing with this puzzle.

Inmates began streaming in through the doorway. Most of them knew exactly where to go, spotting their loved ones the moment they stepped foot in the room. But one prisoner stopped just inside the threshold, waiting for the guard at the door to direct him where to go.

"Grimes, you're at table three."

Lou and Willow tensed. Suddenly, Lou felt ill-prepared. The man walking over to them was huge. He was the epitome of brute force, all muscles and not an ounce of sympathy in his expression.

She glanced at his hands. Free. Why had she expected him to be handcuffed, to have chains holding him back from hurting anyone? Easton had mentioned they couldn't prove any of the more brutal attacks had been him, so he was here, at a lower-security prison. Panic washed through her, making her flush with the heat of her fear.

A sly smirk stretched across Fitz Grimes's mouth as he sank into the seat across from them. "Ladies, to what do I owe the pleasure?"

Lou gaped at the man.

Willow, thank goodness, maintained both her composure and her ability to speak. "Based on that smirk, I have a feeling you know exactly who we are and why we're here, Mr. Grimes, but I'll humor you. It has something to do with your old boss."

While Lou was proud of her friend's grit, she wasn't completely sure antagonizing the man was the best course of action. Clearing her throat, she said, "Mr. Grimes, we know you won't talk to the police about this, but we're hoping you might be more inclined to chat with us about the group you used to be a part of."

"Who's saying I'm not still part of it?" He leaned back in his chair.

Wetting her lips, Lou said, "Fine. Whether or not that's true, people from the group known as the Muscle Car Mafia are being murdered. We thought you might like to help us figure out why."

He chuckled, a sound as rough as sandpaper. "I have a feeling you know exactly why they're being murdered," he said, holding her gaze as he used the same phrasing as Willow had moments before. Leaning forward just a bit, he considered Willow and added, "How is the good detective these days? You know, when he was chasing us around, he was just a lowly officer. Now he's got a detective's badge and a pretty girl on his arm. I'd say he's doing well for himself. Too bad he has so much to lose."

Willow tensed, but Lou grabbed her hand under the table, squeezing it tight to communicate that she could take it from here. Willow had been strong before when Lou hadn't known what to say. Now it was Lou's turn to be the strong one.

"It doesn't bother you that members of your group are killing each other for the chance to be the one to take out Detective West?" Lou asked, ignoring his taunts about Willow and Easton's personal life, though the realization that he knew so much about Easton made her skin crawl with discomfort.

Grimes's shoulders bobbed. "Must be a lot of money on the line. I wouldn't know. I don't know anything." He said the last part louder, his focus cutting to one of the guards over in the corner.

Lou, who was observant at the best of times but had also spent the week working on deductive reasoning puzzles, noticed the interaction. "You're scared."

Surprise flashed across Fitz's features but was quickly replaced by indifference. It was a mask.

"You don't want it to get back to Chevelle that you talked, in case one of these guards is in his pocket. If he found out, you might end up like Bex Mason," Lou whispered, studying his reaction to the name.

His tight jaw didn't give her the definitive answer she wanted. Neither did him saying, "Hmmm, I don't know that name. Is she another of the casualties in this competition you think is happening?"

A smirk curved across Lou's mouth. "Sorry, you probably only knew her as Mustang, but her mistake that night got Chevelle arrested. She paid for it with her life. If he finds out you're talking, even in here, you'll join her. Won't you?"

Fitz swallowed, the muscular cords in his neck tightening with the motion. "I don't know what you're talking about," he reiterated slowly, as if she might not have understood him the first time.

"Sure you don't." Now it was her turn to sit back smugly.

She produced the puzzle from her bag, showing it to the nearest guard first before flattening it on the table. "Tyson Krate, Cobra, was stabbed by someone trying to keep him from collecting the money Chevelle is offering for Easton's murder. Bex Mason was killed by someone in the group for making the mistake that cost Chevelle his freedom. It could've been you, especially with your penchant for violence, GTO."

His knuckles cracked as he clenched his fingers into fists. "So you know my nickname. Big deal." But his indifferent mask dropped for a moment as he noticed the puzzle. "What is that?"

"How we're going to find out the identity of each of your friends and let them join you in here," Willow said tightly.

But Lou knew his question was more basic than that. "It's a grid logic puzzle. It uses deductive reasoning to figure out relationships between things."

And while Lou hadn't been able to find a speck of similarity between herself and the man sitting before her until that moment, the flicker of interest in his expression was one she recognized.

"Are you a fan of puzzles?" Lou took out the puzzle book she'd been toting around with her all week. It felt wrong to make small talk with someone who'd been talking so cavalierly just minutes ago about murder, especially the potential hit on one of her friends. But she also knew she needed his cooperation, and she would use any tools at her disposal in order to earn his trust.

"There's only so many push-ups and sit-ups a guy can do. I needed something else to keep me busy. Puzzles fit the bill." Grimes eased back in his seat.

Swallowing, Lou planned out her next words carefully. She

was finally getting somewhere with the man, and she didn't want to ruin it.

"You use the grids to keep track of your clues and make deductions that lead you to the correct answers." She tapped the puzzle she had made. "See, I know there were six members of the Muscle Car Mafia. I know they each had a nickname after a muscle car, they each had a signature way to steal cars, and they obviously each have a real name."

Grimes's eyes flashed with intrigue. "And what are the circles and Xs for?"

Lou gestured to the row with his name. "The O means that there's a match. I know your name is Fitz Grimes, and that you went by GTO in the group. Since you're the only one who can have that nickname, I put Xs along the rest of this column, since no one else is GTO. And I also know that you can't be any of the other nicknames now, so I put Xs across the rest of the row."

He cocked an eyebrow. "And I used violence to steal cars?" Grimes pushed down on his knuckles, cracking them in a series of quick pops as he nodded toward the O Lou had put across from his name in the section where their signature methods were listed.

"Yeah," Lou scoffed. "That one wasn't too hard to figure out, since you're already in prison for assault."

A snort left him, sounding more amused than intimidating. Lou felt like this puzzle conversation might just be loosening him up.

"You're wasting your time," he said, flattening all her hopes.

Willow pushed back from the table. "No, *you're* wasting our time. Easton was right, Lou. Let's go."

But before she could stand, Grimes jerked his chin toward the puzzle. "That section there shouldn't be our real names. There's no way you're going to find out about those until it's too late. Chev's the only one who knew them, and there's no way he's giving out any of that information."

Biting her lip, Lou saw the truth in his statement. If they kept with the current pattern, not finding out their real names unless they were dead or imprisoned, they'd likely be too late to help Easton.

"What should I put there instead?" Lou asked, poising her pen over the page.

Grimes lowered his voice. "Weaknesses. I may not have known the names of the other members, or even what they looked like, since he made us wear masks anytime we were on a job or met as a group, but I made sure I knew how to take them out if I ever needed to." He tapped his temple.

"Weaknesses?" Lou breathed out the question, fingers hesitating to write anything. "Are you going to tell me what they are?"

He cocked his head. "That depends. What can you do for me?"

Willow scoffed, but Lou didn't let her speak up. "What do you need? Puzzles? I can see if I can leave this book for you. I'm not sure what the rules are about stuff like that, but I'm sure the guards will let me leave it if they can inspect it first. And I have plenty where that came fr—"

"Cool it," Grimes said, interrupting her. "I don't need any of your puzzle books." His throat went taut as he swallowed. "My mom. I'm all she's got. She's got a bad back, and ever since I've been locked up, she's alone. She gets around okay, but it would be nice to have someone check in on her from time to time, to make sure she doesn't need any help around the house. That kinda stuff." He coughed in discomfort, his gaze falling to the table in front of him.

Lou regained her composure. She glanced at Willow, who was regarding Fitz with renewed interest. His mom. That was definitely a surprise.

"Uh, sure." Lou wet her lips. "Yeah, I'd be happy to check on your mom for you."

For the first time since he'd stepped into the room, Fitz Grimes's smile wasn't something to be feared. "I talk to her on the phone every day. I'll give her the information you need. As long as you go to see her, she'll tell you the answers to your little puzzle."

Excitement warred with doubt in Lou's heart. This felt entirely too good to be true. But Lou guessed she wouldn't know unless she tried.

"Where does your mom live?" she asked, pulling the puzzle toward her so she could write the address.

But the guards called out, telling them their time was up.

Fitz stood. "Off Textile Road, by Button Lake. She's in the yellow house. You can't miss it. Number 5320. Her name is Gloria." He was a new man. His gray eyes almost sparkled as he checked over his shoulder before disappearing back down the hallway toward his cell.

Lou returned the puzzle to her bag, standing with Willow.

"Well, we technically didn't get any information out of him, just a promise that his mom will tell us. That could've gone better," Willow said.

But Lou clutched her purse tighter, knowing the puzzle was safe within. "Yeah, but it also could've gone worse."

CHAPTER II

After debating whether to go straight to Fitz's mom's house or give it a day, Lou and Willow decided on the latter. Once that was agreed upon, the drive back to Button from the prison was silent as Lou and Willow digested what they'd learned.

But the silence in the car was quickly shattered as they drove by Willow's and Easton's houses.

"They have *got* to be kidding," Willow said with a groan, clicking her turn signal to take a right onto Pattern Drive instead of continuing on Spool Avenue.

Lou sucked in a breath as she clenched her teeth in a cringe.

There, sitting in front of the rental house, was a couch. Propped on its cushions was a piece of cardboard with the word FREE written in black marker. Next to the couch sat a bookshelf that was obviously broken, probably beyond repair, with a FREE sign taped to the one shelf still intact.

Willow pulled into the driveway, gravel spitting off the tires as she gunned the accelerator up to the rental house. Lou didn't ask questions, she just followed Willow as she got out of the car and stomped up to the porch. The force of her knock on the front door practically rattled Lou's teeth. Lou guessed Willow's choice to knock instead of ringing the doorbell had to do with the physical release that it brought, helping her expend just enough of her angry energy to keep her cool as Rachel answered the door.

"Willow!" Rachel's eyes went wide. "What are you doing here?" Her question was loud enough that Lou could tell she was trying to get her husband's attention wherever he was in the house.

Willow stabbed a finger toward the couch and bookshelf. But before she could say anything, Micah came gliding up to the door like a kid showing his friends how far he could slide on linoleum in socks.

"Willow, hey!" His neck was red, and his gaze bounced between his landlord and the couch. "We thought you'd be at work. What are you doing home?"

The muscles in Willow's jaw tightened as she clenched her teeth. "I have an employee now. He's watching the nursery while I had lunch with Lou."

Lou wasn't surprised that Willow had left out their visit to the prison. If the renters were already worried about the police presence and crime scene next door, she wouldn't want to give them more proof that she was getting further involved in the case.

"An employee!" Rachel said with a big smile. "We didn't know you'd hired someone. That's great. What's his name?"

"Quincy," Willow ground out, obviously unhappy about being pandered to. She wasn't about to be distracted by talk of her employee.

"Oh, I'm so glad. I know you were stressed about leaving the nursery. He came just at the right time. Quincy sounds great." Rachel was too happy about Quincy, and she seemed to realize that it was coming off as fake because she pressed her lips together.

Micah ducked his head. "We're thrilled for you … and Quincy. Um, so what did you want to talk to us about?" He smiled, as if he hoped that might delay the inevitable.

But Willow was not to be deterred—not to mention that her finger was still pointed at the couch, having never dropped as they'd attempted to distract her. "You cannot put garbage on the side of the road like that."

Rachel's mouth formed a small O. "Is it against some kind of town ordinance? I'm sorry. We didn't know."

At that, Willow gritted her teeth together. "Well, no. It's not technically against any laws," she admitted with great difficulty. "But it's an unspoken rule that if you have furniture you don't want anymore, you should either take it to the local donation site or the dump." After a calming breath, Willow motioned to the blue house on the corner of the next road and added, "Mr. Moore was worried enough when we mentioned we would have renters moving in. We don't want to give him any room to complain to the town council about us. Plus, with how much it rains around here, that couch is more likely to get waterlogged than picked up by anyone."

Micah raised his hands. It turned out to be a confusing gesture to use because it made Lou assume he was about to apologize, to say they'd take the couch and bookshelf to the proper donation and dumping sites. Instead, Micah said, "I don't really see how a grumpy neighbor is our problem."

Anger flashed in Willow's eyes, and Lou wondered if she

was about to growl when the screeching of tires interrupted her reaction. Lou and Willow turned to see a truck stopped in the middle of Pattern Drive. A group of college-aged young men spilled out of the cab, swarming around the couch, chattering excitedly.

They froze as they noticed the four people standing on the porch. As if the guys were worried the couch's owners might change their mind, they broke into quick movements, hefting the couch off the ground and into the bed of the truck. Then, to Lou's astonishment, they came back to study the bookshelf. One of the guys mentioned something about how it would fit their gaming system, and the guys tossed it into the truck, along with the couch.

Tires squealed as the driver unnecessarily peeled away.

Willow's lips were parted in disbelief. Micah and Rachel wore matching smug grins.

"Looks like it worked out just fine." Rachel studied Willow as if she pitied her and the position she'd gotten herself in. She grabbed the door, sending a clear message about their conversation being over.

Lou hooked her arm through Willow's. "Looks like it did," she said, knowing her friend wouldn't have the capacity to speak. She tugged Willow off the porch and toward her car.

They sat in tense silence for a moment in the car before Willow pressed down on the ignition. "It was a lucky fluke," she grumbled as she reversed down the driveway, backing toward her house to change their direction before continuing toward the road.

Lou laughed. "Come on. You remember those days when we were in college. Free furniture was like gold."

A smiled tugged reluctantly at the corner of Willow's

mouth, growing in measure with the distance she was putting in between them and her renters. "I mean, I wasn't going to college in New York City, like you, so I wasn't quite as broke and desperate."

"Good point," Lou conceded.

Because she and Ben had met in college, when they were desperately low on funds, they often felt like it was a dream when they were able to afford a condo by Central Park later in their careers. And even though their condo was larger than both of their college apartments combined, Willow's three-bedroom home had felt positively palatial the first time they'd visited her in Button.

Any evidence of her recent frustrations gone, Willow parked in front of Whiskers and Words. "I have a little longer until I've gotta be back to give Quincy his break. Want me to grab us lunch since we missed out on food in favor of our prison visit?"

"That sounds wonderful." Lou's stomach had been growling ever since they'd left the prison, and she'd been planning on grabbing a granola bar from upstairs to eat while she reopened the shop.

Turning off the car, Willow nodded. Lou headed for the bookshop, and Willow jogged across the street to grab some sandwiches from the Bean and Button. Ruby had officially taken over the coffeehouse, and she'd added some tasty food options to the menu in her new role as owner.

Lou flipped the sign in the front door and removed the handwritten note she'd taped there, letting customers know she would be back after a lunch outing. No customers raced inside over the next few minutes, proving there hadn't been anyone waiting with bated breath for books in her absence.

In fact, Lou was still without customers minutes later. She went to check on NF, finding him curled up in one of the office beds, purring almost as loudly as he'd growled at her the day before. Not wanting to disturb him if he was feeling more comfortable, Lou tiptoed out of the office.

Willow returned with their food a short while later. Lou met her friend at the table, pushing aside books and scanning the space for Sapphire, since he wasn't in his usual spot. She found him asleep on one of the fleece beds tucked into an open space on a bookshelf in the mystery section.

The front door jangled open the moment Lou opened her mouth to take the first bite of her sandwich. She hesitated, ready to jump up to help the customer who entered, but noticed it was George. The young woman waved a hand toward her, telling her to stay seated. She flopped onto the third chair at the table.

"Everything good?" Lou asked. She didn't dare take a bite yet since George appeared to have something important to say despite her dismissive hand gesture.

George squeezed her eyes shut for a few moments. When she opened them, she said, "Yeah, sorry. I just had a whole ordeal with my Dungeons and Dragons group."

Lou and Willow didn't need to ask for details. The interested expressions they wore coaxed the information out of George.

"Well, we had our first local tournament this morning," she told them.

"How'd it go?" Willow asked, but cringed halfway through the question as she realized the answer was probably not great if George had called it an ordeal.

Swiping a hand over her forehead, George said, "We've

been planning this for weeks, but apparently no one was on the same page about the details like I thought they were. Phil told people to be at the middle school gym at nine this morning, Owen said eight at the high school, Leena had them at the high school at nine, Chandler forgot to tell anyone, and Drake didn't even remember it was at one of the schools. He sent people to the library." She exhaled in frustration. "It was a disaster. Less than that, actually. It didn't even happen. We didn't have enough people at any one location or time to make up a tournament."

"Are you sure that's all?" Lou appraised her friend.

George grimaced. "Quashing isn't going as well as I hoped."

"Quashing?" Willow asked after swallowing a bite.

"Her feelings for Wesley," Lou answered, receiving a grateful glance from George.

"Especially since I learned he hates cats." George threw her hands into the air in frustration.

"That's not exactly what he said," Lou mumbled, finally picking up her sandwich.

But George ignored Lou's comment. "You would think that would be enough to stop my feelings for the guy, but they're still in here." She tapped on her chest, as if signaling that it was her heart making all the decisions. If it were up to her head, this wouldn't be an issue.

Willow gazed longingly at her sandwich, like all she really wanted to do was take another bite. Instead, she placed it back on the wrapper and said, "I think what you really need is someone else to take your mind off of him."

George's eyebrows lifted with interest.

Encouraged, Willow kept going. "Right now, he's on your

mind a lot because you don't have anyone else to fill those thoughts. If you truly want to forget about him, give yourself someone else to think about."

"I do. I really want to forget him," George pleaded.

"Then put yourself out there. Go on a date." Willow picked up her sandwich, sure that would settle the matter.

"Easier said than done," George scoffed. "How do you suppose I meet someone in a town that's full of retirees?"

"A dating app?" Lou suggested.

George groaned, shaking her head. "That's how I met Wesley, remember?"

Lou chuckled. "Exactly. The app matched you with someone you ended up liking more than you expected you would. So, let it try again. Hopefully, this time it'll find you someone who likes cats and who doesn't make you so"—she motioned toward George, wiggling her fingers—"exasperated."

The young woman considered this advice for a moment. Lou expected her to get up and leave as she had yesterday, but instead of standing, she pulled out her phone.

"Okay, then. You two are going to help me pick my date." George poked at her phone screen, muttering things like "No, too old" and "Not for me" for a minute or two before turning the screen toward Lou. "What about this guy? He's into computers."

Lou took in the picture of the guy on the screen. He appeared to be in his twenties like George and had a big smile. "He looks nice."

George swiveled the phone to face Willow, who gave her a thumbs-up. George pressed something on the screen. "Okay, I told him I want a date. We'll see what happens next."

Willow and Lou congratulated their friend and then turned back to their sandwiches.

"So," George said, "what have the two of you been up to today? Willow, is there a reason you're not at the nursery?"

Willow covered her mouth as she said, "Quincy's watching the nursery for me. As for why … Lou and I just got back from the prison."

George's eyes went wide. "Tell me everything."

CHAPTER 12

It didn't take Lou long to update George on what they'd learned at the prison.

She sat back. "So, you're going to help this guy's mom for information about the other members of the group trying to hurt Easton?"

Lou nodded reluctantly. "He was right. We can't continue working without information about these people. And while his list of weaknesses might be just as unhelpful as everything else we've learned so far, I have to try. With the exception of Grimes, the only way we've been able to learn anything about the other members is when they die."

"And as tempting as it might be to just let them kill each other until there's only one left, I'm worried they'll succeed in getting to Easton one of these times." Willow swallowed thickly, as if the last bite she'd taken of her sandwich wasn't sitting well.

"At least Grimes is in prison," Lou said. "He's the violent one, the one I'd be most worried about hurting Easton. The ones who are left are car thieves. One of them stabbed Cobra, sure, but maybe he made it easy for them. Who knows? This list of weaknesses might help us protect Easton from the ones who are left."

"But you can't get the list from Gloria until tomorrow?" George glanced from Lou to Willow and back again.

Willow shook her head.

"Well," Lou said, "Fitz didn't tell us we had to wait, but we figured he'd need time to call her."

"That makes sense," George said, but the expression on her face was anything but settled. "It just feels like you'll be waiting around, and then what if the information you get from her isn't helpful?"

Willow scooped at the air with her sandwich. "If you've got ideas, bring 'em on. Lou and I are fresh out."

George tapped her fingers on the table as she thought. Charles Lickens took this as a sign that she was calling him over. He jumped up from where he'd been lying by the register and meowed as he jogged toward her.

"Hi, Charles," she said with a laugh, reaching down to pet him as he rubbed up against the legs of her chair. "It's too bad we can't use Easton as bait." George looked up to see Lou and Willow pull horrified faces at her use of that term. "You know? Like, *without* putting him in danger," she amended. "If we could get people to think he's going to be somewhere, maybe we could trap the killer."

Lou crumpled the paper that had been wrapped around her sandwich. She was about to toss it into the garbage when an idea came to her. "George, that's it."

George blinked at the paper balled in Lou's hands as if it held the answer.

Tossing the wrapping, Lou explained, "How do we keep

Easton out of harm's way? We lay a trap of misinformation. Think about your D and D group. They all spread different information. I'm sure it was easy to tell who came at whose invitation based on when and where they showed up. The killers are obviously trying to figure out where and when to strike Easton. Cobra had his schedule written out on that piece of paper in his pocket, remember?"

Willow nodded grimly. How could she forget?

"Well, what if we spread misinformation about where and when Easton will be in certain, vulnerable places, and then situate a patrol there to catch anyone who might show up?" Lou suggested. "Easton won't be anywhere near those areas, of course," she added, hoping to erase the worry from Willow's face.

"And what if the patrols don't catch them?" Willow asked.

Lou thought about that. "If they somehow get away, at least it will help us narrow down who it could be. If we only tell certain people each lie, then we'll know who our suspect pool is, based on which of our fake sites gets hit." Despite Willow's and George's dubious expressions, Lou was feeling more confident about the plan by the second. "We'll need to ask the police for help stationing officers at the different locations."

"I'd bet they'd be happy to do so if it meant they could stop the nighttime surveillance on our house and Easton," Willow said, her tone lifting with excitement. "If Easton agrees, what would we say? Who should we tell?" she asked, proving she needed more information before she agreed to go along with such a plan.

Taking a moment to line up her somewhat scattered thoughts, Lou said, "He's been working on that hazardous-waste-dumping case, right? He said they've been dumping on rural roads. What if we all let it slip where and when Easton might be on a stakeout *alone* at one of these rural locations tonight? We keep track of who we tell about which time and place, so if someone shows up at that location, we know who to question."

"But what if those people tell others?" George asked, bringing up a good point. "You know how this town talks. Someone's bound to share something without realizing."

"Sure," Lou said. "But it's a much smaller pool to ask, and people around here usually remember who they talk to throughout the day."

"If it was between telling the police who I told or being the suspect, I'd definitely choose the former." Willow puffed out her cheeks. Then, as if deciding that was enough, she said, "Okay, let me run this by Easton, but I think we should do it."

AN HOUR LATER, they'd not only secured the blessings of Easton and the Button Police Department, but they'd come up with their different lies.

Willow must've been nervous despite their planning, because she went over the information one more time.

"Lou, you're going to tell anyone you can that you and I are hanging out tonight to keep my mind off the fact that Easton's doing a stakeout at Button Memorial Park, and I'm worried about him being alone." Willow waited until everyone nodded in confirmation before she moved on. "George, you're going to say the same thing, only that the stakeout is going to be on the eastern end of Ribbon Road by the Richards' farm."

"Yes, which will help me leave early from the get-together Phil invited us all to tonight at his house to 'celebrate' the success of our first tournament." She rolled her eyes.

Willow smiled in confirmation. "And I'm pretending I'm getting a phone call from Easton telling me he's going to be doing a stakeout on the old dirt access road off the western end of Spool Avenue from eight to ten." Willow read the information off the note she'd written so she wouldn't forget what she was supposed to say. "The police will have patrols at each of these locations, and they'll question anyone who shows up."

"And we'll all keep lists of who's around each time we mention this information. If they're not local, we jot down as much of a description as we can so the police can track them down later," Lou summarized, knowing that would be important in the event that someone showed at one of the locations but slipped by the police before they could question them.

Willow stuffed the information about her lie in her purse and stood. "Okay. Good luck, everyone. We'll touch base at ten to see if our traps caught anyone."

They agreed. George went to the coffee shop to spread her lie. Willow left for the nursery, and Lou busied herself with straightening the shelves in the bookstore until a grouping of customers wandered in a short while later.

The group was made up of some of the more gossipy local moms, and Lou couldn't help but grin to herself as she recorded their names. Once they made their way to the checkout counter, she asked them what they had planned that evening. They laughed and explained that they were hosting the middle school girls' volleyball team sleepover, so they would need something fun to read.

Just like clockwork, they asked Lou what she had planned

for her Saturday night. *Living in a small town is so predictable,* Lou thought as she spouted off her lie.

"Willow, George, and I are going to have a girls' night since Easton's doing a stakeout to try to find whoever's been dumping hazardous waste."

One of the mom's tsked and said, "I heard about the dumping. How awful. He found it out off Ribbon Road, right? The kids walk that way sometimes after school, and I warned them not to pick up or touch anything on the side of the road, and to report it right away if they saw something like that."

Lou nodded. "Ribbon Road is where he found one of the drops, but he's got a hunch that they might strike Button Memorial Park tonight, so that's where he's going to be from eight to ten. I'm going to keep Willow occupied. You know how she worries about him."

The moms hummed in agreement as they paid. It wasn't as if Lou thought any of them might be in the Muscle Car Mafia, but they would spread that information throughout the town, and Lou trusted they would be able to identify everyone they told if the police came asking later.

Similar iterations of that same conversation happened throughout the rest of Lou's afternoon. By that evening, she had a list of names and felt confident her specific information about Easton's fake stakeout at Button Memorial Park had been properly circulated throughout the town.

Even though Lou's part of the plan was over with, the thought of sitting at home that evening while officers monitored the sites sounded nerve-racking. She needed to get her mind off the case, and she knew just the guy to help her. Pulling out her phone, she dialed.

"What are you doing tonight?" she asked Noah when he answered her call.

Noah chuckled. "Listening to every detail about how your visit to the prison went, over dinner. Sorry, I meant to check in earlier to see how it went, but we had a few emergency appointments show up, and I haven't had a moment to spare until now. I'm just finishing up my notes and a few callbacks, and then I can head your way."

"Sounds great," Lou said. "But I think I'd like to go out for dinner, if that's okay. Sitting around at home might be difficult tonight."

She filled him in on the plan to catch Easton's wannabe killer, and he agreed that going out would be a good way to keep them from pacing through her apartment while they waited for news. Noah suggested that they try the diner she'd gone to the other day with Wesley and Doug.

"Perfect. See you soon." Lou ended the call.

While she waited for Noah, Lou busied herself with brushing the cats. She also spent some time working on bills and placing orders in her office, hoping sharing space with NF might help him warm up to her. While he still growled and hissed anytime she got close, he'd grown comfortable with his office "home" and was usually fast asleep on one of the various cat beds set up in the space each time she poked her head in to check on him. Lou was just bidding the surly cat goodbye as she backed out of the office when Noah arrived.

During the drive out to the remote diner, Lou told Noah all about the trip to the prison, what Fitz had said, and how she was planning on visiting Gloria tomorrow. She also gave him the more detailed version of how their misinformation campaign had come to fruition.

The diner was just as inviting as it had been during her first visit. Between the warm atmosphere and the great company, Lou's worries eased and she sank into the feeling of being with Noah. During that visit to the diner, Lou was able to order for herself and ate more than the few bites she'd taken when she'd sat with Doug and Wesley. The trap they'd set was on her mind, of course, but even with her lingering nervousness surrounding the plan, she felt more relaxed than she had that first visit. It didn't hurt that Noah's arm was wrapped around her before their food arrived, or that his stories about animal antics during appointments that day had her laughing.

In fact, the distraction almost worked so well that Lou just about forgot there was even a police operation going on that evening. Almost. But on their way back into Button, they passed by the access road off Spool Avenue—the location Willow had been assigned to leak. It would've caught Lou's attention anyway, but it became even more interesting when Lou noticed a car coming to a stop at the end of the road. Lou's head snapped around to get a better look at the car as Noah drove past. She checked the time. Nine forty-seven.

"Wait. That was a car at Willow's location. Pull over." She gestured to a wide section of shoulder up ahead.

"Are you sure it wasn't the police?" Noah stared into the rear-view mirror as he brought his truck to a stop.

"I didn't get a good enough look to see," she admitted. Silence enveloped them as they waited, watching for the car to come their way. A shiver passed over Lou after the road remained deserted, save for them. "I don't think they're coming this way."

"Maybe the police already questioned them." Noah's tone dropped low.

"Good point." She took out her phone. "I might just check in with Easton to see."

> Hey, Noah and I just passed the access road off Spool Avenue on our way back from dinner and saw a car. Was it a hit? Did it work?

She tapped her fingers as she waited for his reply. Instead of getting a text back, as she'd expected, Lou's phone rang. Lou jumped at the buzzing sound and cringed at the bright light filling the car.

It was Easton. Lou answered the call, eager to hear an update.

CHAPTER 13

"Easton, hey." She waited, hoping that the fact that he was calling meant that their plan had been successful and it would take too long to type out an explanation of everything that had happened.

"Hey, Lou." Even through the speakerphone, she could hear the strain in Easton's tone.

That only increased her need for the truth. "Noah and I just passed by a car driving down the access road. Was it someone of interest or just a patrol doing a last sweep?"

"Um … neither?" The word was filled with confusion.

The leather of the car seat next to her creaked as Noah leaned closer. Lou shifted the phone toward him.

"Neither?" Lou asked.

"Yeah, we didn't end up posting a patrol at that location. Willow didn't get ahold of you?" He scoffed. "Of course she didn't. She didn't even remember her purse. I'd bet her phone is still sitting in her car," he said to himself more than Lou. "Sorry, Lou. It's been madness. OC has colic."

"Omigosh, how terrifying." Lou gasped.

"I know," Easton said. "Willow got the call as she was putting her stuff away in her office after she left you at the bookstore. She called me on her way and she said she'd let you know, but I'd bet once she arrived at the farm, her attention was completely focused on OC. I should've offered to fill you in, but we've been swamped here too." He exhaled. "Beau went to check on Steve this afternoon because he was making a ton of noise. When he got to the pasture, OC was pacing, grunting, pawing at the ground, and acting weird. Beau and Peggy Lee didn't recognize the signs of colic, but the moment Willow heard, she knew what it was. She told Quincy that she needed to leave as soon as she hung up the call. In her rush, she left her purse behind."

Fear churned in Lou's gut. Colic. Willow talked about the illness as if it were the scariest thing that could happen to a horse. Given how many of her equestrian friends had lost horses to the illness, she assumed it was.

"Is OC okay?" Lou's throat constricted with emotion, but she croaked out the question anyway.

"Yes." Easton exhaled the word with a mountain of relief. "She thinks they caught it in time, thanks to Steve. She told Beau to walk him until she got there, and not to let him roll around, so he wasn't much worse for wear by the time she arrived."

Lou remembered Willow saying that the worst thing that could happen when a horse had colic was for them to roll around and get their organs all twisted up inside.

"She took over the walking until the vet arrived, but she hasn't left his side since. I'm just about to go see her. Anyway, all that's to say that Willow didn't get a chance to plant her misinformation before she raced out to the farm to be with him, so her site is dead. Which was a good thing because we got a call about a car in a ditch about an hour ago and needed a patrol to help with that issue."

Digesting the information, Lou said, "Wait. But if Willow didn't have time to plant her information and that wasn't a police car patrolling the site, who did Noah and I just see driving down the road?" A chill wound through her, causing her to shiver.

In the darkness of the car, she studied Noah. The shadows deepened as he furrowed his brow with the same questions.

"I don't know." Easton hesitated. "Maybe it's just a random person."

"Out for a drive down a dead-end service road on a random Saturday evening during freezing February temperatures?" Noah's question came out, flattened by disbelief.

A thoughtful "Hmmm" came from Easton.

"Maybe it's your hazardous-waste dumper, Easton. Should we go back and see if we can catch them?" Lou asked, her heartbeat quickening at the thought.

But Easton's answer came instantly. "Absolutely not. There's no way a patrol will get there in time since they're still on-site with the car in the ditch, and I don't want you putting yourself in jeopardy. We're just going to have to let this one go. No one showed at the other locations, so I think this has to be a random coincidence. You should go home."

"Oh, there's no way I'm going home."

Noah's eyes slid to her, only visible in the small amount of light from the phone screen. Easton seemed stunned into silence.

"We're heading to the farm to be with Willow," she

amended, realizing how alarming her first statement must've sounded.

"Okay. See you there." Easton's words were tinged with a certain lightness, as if he were smiling at himself. He hung up, and Lou slid her phone back into her purse.

"So that car was there for some other reason? That's odd," Noah whispered as they stared in his rear-view mirror again. No cars had passed by, which meant that the vehicle must've turned the opposite direction, heading away from Button.

"Very." A shiver raced up the backs of Lou's arms. "Sorry, I kind of volunteered you to come with on the phone. You can drop me off at home so I can drive myself if you don't want to join me."

"Oh, I'm coming with," Noah checked the road again before he pulled a U-turn and started back in the direction they'd come, toward Milton Farm and Willow.

The access road was deserted and dark when they passed by the second time and Lou's mind buzzed with questions. But any thoughts of cars or access roads disappeared the moment they arrived at the farm. Easton's car was parked next to Willow's in front of Peggy Lee's white farmhouse. Lou and Noah bypassed the house, however, rushing to the left toward the barn.

The door was open just a crack, enough to let people pass in and out, but not enough to let out too much of the heat. Peggy Lee and Beau stood just outside one of the stalls, concern etched in their serious expressions. Beau must've left his Pomeranian, Mr. Muffins, inside because the small dog wasn't in the young man's arms as usual.

The earthy aromas of hay, dirt, and horse curled around

Lou in the space as they stepped forward and peered into the stall. Willow followed Easton as he walked around OC, running a hand along his back as they checked him over. The horse's head hung low, as if he were completely drained; it was such a difference from his normally attentive state. His breath came in rapid puffs and pants, rather than the steady rhythm Lou was used to, showing the pain he was experiencing.

Steve was being kept in the stall next to OC, but the goat must've gotten the seriousness of the situation because, for the first time, he wasn't making noise or trying to escape.

"Hey," Lou said as they stopped next to Peggy Lee and Beau.

Willow's attention whipped over to the newcomers. Tears instantly filled her eyes as she rushed to meet them. Lou wrapped her arms around her best friend, squeezing tight as her shoulders shuddered with a fresh round of sobs. Being someone who couldn't watch others cry without doing so herself, Lou's vision blurred, and she gripped Willow tighter.

"He's okay. He's going to be okay," Lou whispered, hoping to soothe her friend's fears.

Willow's tears were probably more of a release of pent-up worries at that point than fear for OC's life, but Lou wasn't one to judge. Easton wasn't the only one who'd had a stressful week, and this was the last thing Willow probably expected to deal with.

Stepping back, Willow bowed her head a touch, as if she couldn't commit to a full nod.

"What did Dr. Standhour say?" Noah asked, using the name of Willow's equine-specific veterinarian.

"She said it doesn't appear to be anything he ate. Her

assessment was that it was probably the stress of moving from my barn to this one."

Noah didn't question the equine veterinarian's diagnosis. Other than studying horses in college, he didn't have a ton of current experience; his practice treated small animals, mostly cats and dogs. He would check OC out every once in a while when he got a cut or had a small issue, but Willow's main vet was a mobile unit, working out of Mount Vernon and specializing in horses.

"The vet gave him Banamine for the pain and Buscopan to help with the colic. She prescribed some laxatives that I can pick up tomorrow if he's still not doing better. I'm going to see if he wants to walk again in a bit. I'm just giving him a bit of a rest since he's been going nonstop for a while." She glanced at Noah to get his assessment.

He stepped forward, asking Willow a few questions as he checked out the horse. Willow answered everything in extreme detail. Her love for OC was always clear, but Lou's throat tightened at how she'd committed every single thing the vet had said to memory, as if forgetting anything would mean the difference between life and death for her equine best friend.

When the horse began fidgeting again, groaning in discomfort and acting as if he might try to roll, Noah and Easton took a turn walking him out in the field. Panic flashed across Willow's features for a moment once OC was out of her sight, but she trusted Noah and Easton. Relaxing, she turned to Lou.

"What do you need? What can I do?" Lou asked, wanting nothing more than to be helpful to her friend.

Willow regarded Lou. "Just you being here is enough. Getting to hug you made all the difference. But really, don't feel like you have to stay much longer. I know it's late. I'm going to stay here tonight. Peggy Lee has a camping cot I can sleep on, and a sleeping bag I can borrow. I'll sleep in the barn with OC just to make sure he's past it all."

Lou expected nothing less. She also knew Peggy Lee would take care of them, doting on Willow and checking on the two of them throughout the night.

The clomping of hooves preceded Noah, Easton, and OC as they reentered the barn a few minutes later.

"I think that Banamine kicked in." Noah motioned toward the horse, who was licking and breathing deeply. "He's feeling calmer."

Willow was by his side in an instant, rubbing a hand down his neck and praising him for getting through the worst of it. They got the horse settled back into his stall, and Noah even mentioned that Steve could rejoin him since things were looking up.

The relief to see OC was doing well overwhelmed Lou so much that she almost forgot to ask Willow about the car they'd seen.

"Oh, Easton, did you have time to ask Willow about the car?" Lou chewed on her lip as she looked from the detective to her best friend.

Willow's forehead creased in confusion, but Easton's eyes flew open wide.

"I totally forgot. Sorry, Lou." Easton shook his head as if his thoughts weren't lining up correctly and he needed a physical shake-up to fix it. "Lou and Noah saw a car at your location, but I told them you didn't have time to plant the information so it had to be a coincidence."

Willow let out a groan. "I'm so sorry. Yeah, I didn't get the chance to plant the lie at all."

"No worries." Lou didn't want her friend to feel bad about anything else tonight.

Willow's tired brain seemed to catch up. "But you saw a car?"

They explained everything they'd seen.

"Weird," Willow said. "I didn't tell anyone, so it must've been a random visitor."

They agreed and returned to Lou's car, driving back to Button. The apartment felt odd without Willow there that night, giving Lou a sick feeling in her stomach.

Checking her phone, Lou noticed that she'd missed a few texts from George.

> Hey, weren't the police going to check in with us? I haven't heard anything.

> I can't get a hold of Willow either.

> Is everything okay?

Lou dialed George's number. "Hey," she said when her friend picked up. "Yeah, it's a long story. I figured it would be best to tell you over the phone."

CHAPTER 14

"Everything okay with Willow?" Silas asked the next morning as he bustled through the front door of Whiskers and Words, a newspaper stuck under one arm, his signature bowler cap secure on his head. "I noticed the nursery was closed this morning on my walk in."

Lou took a breath before answering, knowing the explanation was going to be on the longer side. "Yes and no," she said to start.

The rest of the regulars, already settled around the shop, stopped what they were doing to gape in Lou's direction. Well, all but George, who already knew the entire story.

"OC got a case of colic, which the vet thinks is in response to the stress of moving from his normal barn to Milton Farm," Lou started.

"Colic? Isn't that just a bad stomach?" Cricket asked, obviously not understanding why that would be cause for alarm.

"In people, yes," Lou said. "But horses can't throw up, and their digestive systems can get blocked or twisted. If that happens, colic can become fatal." Lou hoped she was describing it all correctly. "Anyway, she raced out of the nursery the moment she heard yesterday and is keeping it closed today so she can stay with him out at Peggy Lee's place."

The gravity of the situation settled over Cricket. Silas and Forrest adopted similar countenances, knowing how much the horse meant to Willow.

"Any news from her this morning?" George asked from where she sat on the floor, letting Geralt socialize with the other cats for a few minutes, free from his wrap.

"Not so far, but I'm guessing no news is good news." Lou smiled softly.

"Does Willow need us to grab her purse from the nursery and bring it out to her?" George asked. "I have time before I meet with the D and D group this afternoon."

Lou's eyebrows moved closer to her hairline. "You know what? I don't know. Maybe I'll text Easton and see." She grabbed her phone and sent him a message with the question.

They didn't have to wait long to hear back. A few moments later, a response came through from Easton.

That would be amazing, actually. I went by last night, but Quincy had already locked up and left by the time I made it there. He's been using our spare set of keys, so George would need to go by his place to grab them. I can send her his number.

George got Geralt situated into his carrier once more while Lou finalized the plan with Easton and Quincy, texting him and getting his address for George as well as giving him a heads-up she was going to swing by. Once she had the keys, she could open Willow's office and grab her purse.

And Lou thought that would be the last she saw of her friend until later that afternoon when her Dungeons and Dragons group met at the bookshop for their regular Sunday session. But George wandered into Whiskers and Words only a half hour later while Lou was helping a customer. Geralt was no longer strapped to her chest, but Willow's purse hung from her right arm. Even after the customer Lou was ringing up paid and left, George didn't make eye contact with Lou. She paced, staring off into the middle distance.

"Everything okay?" Lou asked warily. "Did you want me to drop that off with Easton at the station?"

George swallowed. "Quincy," she croaked out the name. "What do we know about him?"

"Quincy?" Lou blinked. "Quincy's the best. He's been a lifesaver to Willow."

"And he just showed up within the last two weeks asking for a job?" George placed a hand on her hip. "Pretty suspicious, if you ask me."

"Where's this coming from, George? Did he say something to you when you went to get the keys?"

George shook her head, but stalked toward Lou, setting Willow's purse down on the check-out counter in between them. "When I went into Willow's office, her purse was open, like this."

She slipped her arm out from under the strap and opened the floppy purse so its contents were on display. Willow always carried huge, baggy purses, and she had a bad habit of filling them with things she probably didn't need. As if proving Lou's point, a pair of pruning sheers and two seed packets sat next to Willow's wallet inside her purse currently.

Lou couldn't see where George was going with this until

she said, "The note Willow wrote herself about the lie she was supposed to tell about where Easton was going to be last night was sitting just like that." George motioned to the sticky note clinging to Willow's wallet.

Easton stakeout. Old forest service access road off Spool Avenue. 8-10pm

"And that's the only location where anyone showed up," George said.

Lou chewed on her lip. "But Willow never told anyone. She got called away right when she arrived at the nursery after leaving here. And no customers are allowed in her office, so no one would've seen the note." Lou's lungs jolted as she filled them to capacity. "Except Quincy."

"Exactly," George said, seeing that she finally understood.

"We have to tell Easton." Lou's eyes snapped up to meet George's.

Easton did a double take as Lou and George entered his office a few minutes later. "Oh, I thought it was just going to be George." His eyes cut to Willow's purse.

The women sat in the chairs across from his desk.

"I closed the bookshop because we need to tell you something." Lou's fingers gripped the handle of Willow's purse tight as she waited for Easton to let them know he was ready to listen.

George saw that as her cue to take over the story. "I think

Quincy was the one Lou and Noah saw driving down that dead-end road last night."

When Easton gave her an incredulous look, George went into detail, repeating everything she'd told Lou. The hard set to the detective's jaw softened as she presented the facts.

"The last thing," George said. "His tires were pretty muddy. Well, the wheel wells surrounding them were."

That part was news to Lou.

George must've recognized Lou's confusion. "I only just remembered thinking it was odd. But he got the keys out of his car for me, and I noticed the mud while I stood there. He lives in an apartment complex. There wouldn't be a reason for his wheel wells to be caked with mud unless…"

"Unless he was the one who was driving up and down the unpaved access road last night." Easton's neck went taut after he finished the statement for her. "Quincy?" he whispered, his disbelief palpable.

Lou brought out her logic puzzle, tapping her finger on the section where she'd listed the Muscle Car Mafia's signature car-stealing methods. "One of the open spots is an infiltrator. What if Quincy is the member of the group who was known for playing the long game? What if he thought the best way to get to you was actually to get close to Willow instead?"

Even mentioning it made Lou feel sick. If it was true, had Quincy's plan been to hurt Willow or just learn about Easton's movements and habits from the person who knew him best? Lou didn't know if she was ready to learn the answer.

Easton ran a hand down his face. "Do you think he caught onto what you suspected, George?"

"No, mostly because I didn't suspect anything until after I got the keys from him and went to pick up her purse. I'm honestly surprised that he didn't move the sticky note or cover it up. It was so obviously out in the open."

"He didn't know it was a trap. He has no idea that any of us saw him on that access road last night," Easton said, concentrating on Lou. "Did you learn anything from Grimes' mom that might help us here?"

"I haven't gone yet. Between everything with Willow and OC…"

Easton's blue eyes bore into Lou. "Is there any way you can go now? Is the bookshop okay being closed for a little longer? I wouldn't normally ask, but I need to know if there's anything she can tell us that might strengthen our case before I bring it to the chief."

"Yes, I can go now. It's been slow today, so the shop should be fine." Checking her watch, Lou sucked in a pained breath and turned to George. "Oh, but we're getting close to the start of your D and D group. I might not be back in time."

"Why don't you drop me off and unlock the shop for me, and I'll look after the place while you're at Gloria's," George offered. "My role this week means I won't have a problem jumping up to help customers if it comes to that."

Lou loosed a relieved sigh. "That sounds perfect. Thank you."

With a wave to Easton, the women left. Lou unlocked Whiskers and Words and left George behind as she drove toward Button Lake, hoping Gloria Grimes would have the answers they desperately needed.

CHAPTER 15

itz Grimes had oversold how easy it would be to find his mother's house. *You can't miss it?* Wrong. Lou, in fact, missed it the first three times she drove by.

Two factors contributed to her inability to find the house. The first was that the houses situated around Button Lake were all set back from the road, at the end of long, gravel driveways, so Lou only had the house numbers on their mailboxes to go by. None of them had 5320 listed anywhere.

Finally, after circling the block a second time, Lou tried her luck on the remaining driveway. The mailbox was so old that the only numbers visible were the 5 and the 0, and only because the rest of the plastic was faded around where the numbers used to be.

Armed with the knowledge that 5 and 0 were part of the address she was searching for, the second factor that caused Lou to doubt if she was in the right place was that the house at the end of that driveway wasn't technically yellow, as Fitz had described it. Its greenish tint made Lou ease her foot onto the brake and reach for the gearshift so she could back up without being seen, obviously in the wrong place. But as she looked closer, she realized the house *used* to be yellow. The siding was just covered in a thin layer of moss.

Lou regulated her erratic breathing as she parked. She had no idea what to expect as she left the safety of her car and headed for Gloria Grimes's house, which meant she would need to keep her wits about her.

Knocking on the front door, Lou heard a scratchy voice call out, "It's open!"

Many aromas hit Lou as she opened the door and stepped inside the house, none of them pleasant. She didn't care to identify any of the specific scents, knowing it would take a deeper breath to do so, and Lou was content to take quick, shallow sips of air inside the musty space.

The visual she was met with was just as overwhelming as the smell of the place. Clutter gathered on almost every surface. Cans were stacked all over the kitchen counters to Lou's right. Old paperbacks littered a dining room table, and the couch—well, that was covered with cats. Ah, so that was one of the smells.

At least six cats curled on a scratched and torn blue couch to Lou's left. Because there were a few curled up asleep together, Lou couldn't get an accurate count without moving closer. Before she could, movement in the corner of the room caught her eye. A small woman sat in a worn recliner next to the cat couch.

A flash of pink washed over the woman's cheeks before she glanced down. Lou felt her embarrassment like a punch to the gut. Gloria must've recognized what her house looked like.

But the woman's self-consciousness either passed or she

buried it deep, because she lifted her chin in defiance and said, "You must be the busybody my son warned me about."

Her voice had a croaky quality to it, like a cartoon frog. The scratchiness gave Lou the impulse to want to clear her throat. She quelled the urge and smiled instead.

"That's me. I'm Louisa Henry." If this woman thought she was going to scare her away with insults, she was going to be disappointed. "I'm taking the fact that you were expecting me as confirmation that he called with the information I need."

Gloria wet her lips. "He did."

Her skin was wrinkled, and her hair was still dark, like her son's, but gray twined its way through the strands Lou could see before they were gathered into a braid behind her back.

"But I have some questions of my own before I hand it over."

Gloria didn't gesture for Lou to sit, but Lou pulled a dining room chair over—the only one that wasn't stacked with boxes. As she moved it, Lou noted that a small space had been left clear at the table next to the unencumbered chair. At least she had a place at the table to eat.

Gloria's jaw tightened. "What do you want with my son?" she asked once Lou had settled.

The question, though brusque, quaked with so much emotion that Lou felt herself rock back in her chair a little in shock. Gloria transformed in front of her. No longer a crotchety woman who wanted to shut out the world, she was a mother worried about her son.

"Only information, I promise. I think something he knows about this group he used to work with might help save my friend's life." Lou hoped Gloria might recognize some of the same emotion and worry for those she loved in her own statement.

Her dark eyes flashed, showing that she had.

"My friend, Detective West, is in trouble." Lou placed her hands in her lap. "Chevelle Hayes is convinced he's the one thing standing in his way of being granted parole, and we think he's put a hit out on him to clear his path to freedom. He's summoned the group known as the Muscle Car Mafia to do so, offering a lot of money. Your son knows things about that group that might help us identify who they are before they can hurt the detective."

Gloria mimed spitting on the floor to her left. One of the cats on the couch jumped at the sound. Lou braced herself to hear a diatribe about Detective West and how he was the reason her son had been taken away from her.

But instead, she said, "That Chevelle has always been a slimy creep. I warned Fitzy against getting involved with him and his group." Sadness tugged at the corners of her mouth. "He's not bad … my boy." Her pleading gaze met Lou's. "He just got caught up in making money the wrong way. He didn't know how to get out."

Lou thought back to those brief glimpses of fear he'd shown her during their chat at the prison. That, plus his obvious care for his mother, made her feel like Gloria told the truth. "I believe you. And I don't want to put him in any more danger. I just need to know if he can help me keep Chevelle from hurting anyone else."

Gloria smacked her lips as she considered that. After a moment, she selected a piece of paper from a small stack on the crowded end table next to her chair. "Here's the information he told me to give you." Her knobby fingers shook as she held it out.

Jumping to her feet, Lou retrieved the note from Gloria. It crackled as she unfolded it. Gloria's handwriting was wobbly, but other than that, her cursive script was beautiful. It was clear to Lou that penmanship was something Gloria took great pride in, and she could see the time and focus the woman still took to keep her hand steady even though it had become harder over the years. Lou's eyes pored over the text.

> Weaknesses of the MCM: needs glasses but is too vain to wear them, bad knee/slow runner, perfectionist, dyslexic, colorblind, asthma.
>
> I'll give you mine for free. I'm dyslexic and have to work really hard to read anything. For clues about the rest, you'll have to come back.

Come back? Did he mean to his mother's home or to the prison? Lou's gaze flicked up to meet Gloria's. From the hard set to her mouth, Lou guessed it was the former.

"I don't need your help, you know," Gloria croaked, confirming Lou's suspicion.

Lou stared back, making a point not to clock everything in the house that needed cleaning or fixing. "Your son helped you a lot before he went to prison, didn't he?" The story Fitz had outlined during their visit filled in. Details became clear.

Gloria's gaze dropped to her lap. Her expression hardened. She was closing off again.

In that moment, Lou thought back to one of her authors from New York City, back when she used to be an editor for a major publishing house. The man, Victor, had been a bestselling author for over a decade, but his wife passed away in the middle of the final book he had contracted with the publishing house. He couldn't finish it. After extension upon extension, Lou paid a visit to Victor's apartment in Brooklyn.

Gloria's home reminded Lou of Victor's apartment in a lot of ways. It was filled with loss and the overwhelming sense of drowning. Minor tasks went undone, and then piled up until they became big problems. An unwashed dish here and there wasn't an issue until there weren't any clean dishes left. Victor had confessed that he just didn't have the energy to clean, let alone write.

So Lou had started with the basics. She'd picked up a washcloth and had started on the dishes. While she worked, she asked Victor about his book, extricating details one by one from the man's once closed-off mind. She returned daily, bringing food to cook him when she noticed he'd stopped doing that as well.

They chatted about his book and his wife as she worked. Victor began to join her, cleaning the kitchen first, and then moving to the living room. And then he stopped cleaning, choosing instead to pull out his laptop and type during her visits. At first, he'd stop a lot, asking Lou's opinion on a plot point or a character choice. But as the days passed, Lou would work on organizing or cooking and Victor would write.

Months later, the man had finished the first draft of his novel. He'd even sold another one, a proposal he'd written up for a book loosely based on him and his wife, their life together.

Lou knew this wasn't quite the same situation. She and Victor had a relationship before that first visit. She'd edited three books for him over the years. They had a trust built up. With Gloria, she was starting from nothing.

So Lou started small.

"What kind of books do you enjoy reading?" she asked, motioning to the stack sitting next to Gloria.

The woman's head lifted slowly. She studied the novels, her appraisal moving from the group next to her to the large amount piled on the dining room table.

"My favorite are Regency romances." A grin lifted the corners of her mouth, showing off the first sign of true happiness Lou had seen since she arrived. "It all started with my love of Jane Austen when I was younger. That's actually where my son's name came from."

"Fitzwilliam," Lou whispered in realization, having incorrectly assumed Fitz to be his full name.

Gloria chuckled. "But I could only reread those books so many times, so I eventually branched out to new authors, and I found I loved reading about lords, dukes, and earls."

Lou mirrored Gloria's grin. "I have a few favorites in that genre as well," she said. "I don't know how much Fitz told you about me, but I run a bookstore. I can bring you some titles ... if you need new material." She added the last statement as her attention roamed over the piles of books. It was quite possible Gloria had enough books to last her a lifetime, and she didn't need anything from Lou.

But Gloria put a hand on her chest. "That would be so wonderful. I've read everything here at least once."

Lou coughed in surprise. "You have?"

As a lifelong reader, Lou's to-be-read list was long and constantly increasing, no matter how quickly she read. It was one of her favorite things about readers. They were some of the most determined people she'd ever met. They could have a list of books they wanted to read as long as a football field, but the moment they heard about a new release or a recommendation from a friend, they'd casually say, "I'll add it to my list" as if it wasn't daunting in the least. To readers, a long list of books to be read was a gift, a challenge, not something to be feared.

Gloria, however, had to be the one reader Lou had ever met who'd read every book in her home.

"Well, then." Lou composed herself, getting over her shock. She eyed Gloria. "It looks like you're a woman in need of some new books. And I might be just the person to help you."

Hope flashed behind Gloria's eyes, and then it was replaced by tears.

CHAPTER 16

Lou was by Gloria's side in an instant, kneeling next to her chair as she placed a supportive hand on the woman's shaking shoulder.

What had started as a few silent tears rushing down her cheeks had quickly devolved into full body sobbing. Gloria had been holding a lot inside for quite a long time, Lou guessed.

"Oh, Gloria. I'm so sorry." Lou kept her voice soft, calm. She waited as the woman sniffed and tried to compose herself.

"It's been so hard without my boy." Her froggy voice sounded fully underwater now, soaked to the bone with heartache. "I try not to worry him. I know he feels awful and blames himself for being locked away, but he kept me going. Without him? I've been having a hard time getting by." Her watery eyes locked on to Lou's. "As I'm sure you can tell from the state of this place."

"Fitz mentioned that your back bothers you," Lou said. "I'm sure it's hard to get around to house chores when you're in pain."

New tears spilled down Gloria's cheeks. "I was a flagger for road construction for twenty-five years. But one evening, when we were working late to avoid the heat of the day, a drunk driver hit me. I was lucky, really. It could've been so much worse. But my back hasn't ever been the same, and I've been out of work since."

Lou listened intently, staying in her kneeling position.

"I blame myself for Fitzy getting involved in that darn group. Money was short, and he was having a hard time finding work that could support us both." Gloria sniffed. "One day he came home with more money than I knew what to do with. When I asked him how he'd gotten it, he said not to worry. I did, of course, and after a few months, I was able to get the truth out of him about the Muscle Car Mafia. He wouldn't stop, even though I begged him. Said it was one of those groups where once you're in, it's a death sentence to get out." She let out a shaky breath. "I had so much hope when that boss of his was arrested."

One of the cats on the couch stood, stretched, and jumped into Gloria's lap, as if it had heard her crying and knew she needed comforting. She stroked its fur absentmindedly as she continued her story.

"He even got a job working at a garage in Kirk once Chevelle was arrested and the jobs dried up. But then I got sick, and the hospital bills were too much. He took one last job with some guys he'd met at the garage." She snorted. "That's what he told me it was going to be. *One last job.* These guys said they knew of a car that could bring in a bunch of money that was just sitting in someone's garage."

"What happened?" Lou asked, remembering Easton saying

that Fitz had been charged with assault, that he'd beat up two guys.

"The idiots didn't mention that the car was sitting in the garage of an elderly man who lived alone. While Fitz was working on stealing it, they 'kept watch' to make sure they weren't discovered." Gloria used finger quotes around the phrase and rolled her eyes in disgust. "Turned out that their way of making sure they weren't caught was to beat up the old man. Fitzy caught them before they could do any major damage to the man, thankfully. He pummeled them both for what they'd done." Gloria jerked her head back and forth. "But the neighbor had called the cops, and when the two idiots with him woke up, they said it was all his idea, that he'd forced them to do all of it. It was their word against his."

Lou wondered if she knew about the awful things he'd done as part of the Muscle Car Mafia. Easton had made it sound like those weren't quite so innocent. She decided to keep that to herself.

The cat in Gloria's lap, a fluffy orange one who purred so loudly Lou almost couldn't hear Gloria, lay down, blinking lovingly up at the woman.

"Fitzy knows he's done things the wrong way," she said, coming to a resigned end to her story. "He said he's using his time to make a better plan, to pay for what he did so he can do things right once he gets out."

They sat in silence for a moment. The only sound was the intense purring of the orange cat.

"Gloria," Lou started. The older woman glanced at her. "What would you say to me coming by a couple of times a week? I could help you cook some meals so you have leftovers to heat up." She didn't need to glance behind her at the mountain of cans to know that the woman probably hadn't been eating anything fresh for a good while. "My significant other is also quite handy around the house. He could help with a few of the things you need done, that Fitz used to take care of for you. He's also a veterinarian. He'll be able to check out your cats to make sure they're staying healthy."

The frown Gloria had worn when Lou first arrived returned. "These cats are my priority. I make sure they're as healthy as can be," she said, biting out the statements defensively.

"I'm sure they are." Lou raised her hands in surrender at that point. "I meant that as more of an in-case-they-get-sick scenario."

Tears returned to Gloria's eyes. "That would be wonderful. It's hard to ask for help, but I know I need it, that I've needed it for a while now. The teenager that delivers my groceries will only put them away for me, but he doesn't stick around because I can't tip that much." Her fingers clasped the arm of her chair in worry.

"I'm not asking for anything in compensation," Lou assured her. "I just want to make sure you have the help you need."

"I guess you can come back, then," Gloria said after a moment, a playful smirk flitting across her face.

"Okay, well, I have a few things to take care of, but I'll be back later today." Lou stood, clutching the paper with the note from Fitz in one hand. "Just to make sure, you don't mind if I bring people to help me?"

Hesitating only for a moment, Gloria said, "No. If you trust them, Louisa, I will too."

"Great." Lou grinned. "I'll see you a little later, then." She turned toward the door.

But before she could leave, Gloria called out, "Fitz calls me every day at five. The note I gave you was from yesterday. I should have new information this evening. I'm sorry that I can't be of more help, but I don't know anything about that group except for the name of his boss. But when Fitzy calls, I'll tell him he'd better give you something good."

Hope filled Lou for the first time that day. "Thank you, Gloria. I'll see you after five, then."

Lou raced from Gloria's house to the police station. The note in her purse felt akin to a lottery ticket. She didn't yet know if its contents were worthless or life-changing.

Easton was waiting for her when she arrived. "Anything?" he asked.

"Maybe?" she told him with a cringe, motioning for him to lead the way to his office.

Easton cleared a place on the edge of the desk, and Lou flattened both the note from Fitz and the puzzle in the space. "Any of these sound like a weakness Quincy might have?"

Running his finger over the list, Easton paused on one word: colorblind. "Quincy's colorblind."

Lou hadn't known that.

But Easton nodded assuredly. "He told Willow up front when she mentioned hiring him. Said he might not be the best with the flowers because he couldn't see the different colors, just shades of gray. She told him that she thought it would be just fine, and that she was impressed with him being up front. She hired him on the spot." The detective let out a humorless laugh. "Truthful," he spat out the word like it was a curse.

"So, you think that Quincy really could be one of these MCM people?" Lou turned toward him.

Easton scratched at his cheek. "Yeah, I do. And I think this is the last piece of information the chief will need to back me on bringing him in for questioning." He tapped the note from Fitz. "Thank you for getting this for me, Lou."

She told him it wasn't a problem and then turned to leave. "Oh, and I'll be heading back to Gloria's tonight, so we'll see if she gets any more information from her son that might be helpful."

Easton's smile fell. "So soon?"

Lou kicked the edge of the desk with the toe of her shoe. "She needs a lot of help. He wasn't wrong that she's been struggling without him."

"Okay." Easton held his hand up in a wave, already moving toward the chief's office. "Good luck with that. I'll let you know what comes of this." He flicked two fingers toward the note, making the paper snap in response.

Lou hoped it was something good. They needed positive news, Willow especially.

Stepping inside her bookshop a short while later, Lou breathed in the calming, cozy scents of the books and the fire George must've started. Lou rarely took her home for granted, but after spending time in Gloria's crowded, musty house, she let herself feel grateful for everything she had in her life. A renewed need to give that feeling back to Gloria ignited inside Lou, urging her forward.

Waving in greeting toward the D and D group chattering toward the back of the shop, Lou set down her purse and went straight for the Regency romance section, picking out a few books to take to Gloria that evening.

CHAPTER 17

Noah was more than happy to accompany Lou to Gloria's house after she closed up the bookshop that evening.

"Should I bring any tools?" he asked when she climbed into his truck after locking up.

"Maybe just make a list of the things you think need to be done. I think tonight's just going to be about cleaning out some clutter and getting her a freshly cooked meal." Lou eyed the bucket of cleaning supplies she'd slipped into the truck bed. They would need to stop by the grocery store for ingredients. "I thought we could start with something simple with a lot of leftovers like that roasted veggie and orzo dish we made the other night."

Noah's expression lit up at the memory. "Oh, that was great. Yeah, she'll have food for days with that meal." He drove them to the store to collect the ingredients.

They also picked up a few simple breakfast options and a few bags of salad that Gloria could easily make for lunches.

When they arrived at the once-yellow house, unloading the

groceries and supplies from Noah's truck, Gloria's greeting was the complete opposite of what it had been earlier when Lou had shown up for the first time. She met them at the door with a smile on her face. She was stiff as she walked, showing them inside, but that she was even up and moving felt like a triumph to Lou.

"Gloria, this is Noah Ramero. Noah, this is Gloria Grimes." Lou made the introductions as she brought the grocery bags into the kitchen. "Gloria, I figured I'd have Noah start with checking out the cats, and then you can help him make a list of stuff you need done around here."

Noah went straight for the couch, where the cats were still congregating. Gloria tottered after him.

Lou stopped short as she entered the kitchen. "Did you do some cleaning?"

The older woman beamed. "I thought I'd make some room so you wouldn't be crowded in there. Most of those cans were empty anyway. I tossed them in the recycling bin. I just felt so energized after you left." Her eyes opened wider. "Oh, and I talked to Fitzy."

At that news, Lou and Noah stopped what they were doing.

"He gave me another note. It doesn't make any sense to me, but I'm hoping you'll be able to decipher it." She grabbed the paper from the table next to her recliner and handed it to Noah.

His eyes narrowed at the page, and he brought it over to Lou, shaking his head to let her know it wasn't making sense to him. Lou wasn't surprised. With him spending the day with Marigold, she hadn't had the opportunity to tell him about the list of weaknesses Grimes had given her yet. She took the paper from him.

A hot-wire expert wouldn't be very good if they were color blind. Someone who stays inside and stares at screens all day wouldn't have to worry about breathing in something that would irritate their lungs.

"Got it. It's two clues to help me figure out which weaknesses go with which MCM member." Neither clue had anything to do with Quincy's involvement in the group, so it wouldn't be something she needed to tell Easton right away.

With the clues safely tucked in her pocket, Lou got to cooking. Noah washed his hands and helped her with the dish once he'd checked out the cats and made a list of repairs Gloria needed.

"Your cats are all in excellent health," he told her as he began chopping onions for the dish.

Gloria lifted her chin higher. "I told you," she said to Lou, showing some of her earlier surliness.

"You did. You were right," Lou conceded, shooting Noah a quick grin.

Noah took over finishing the meal while Lou and Gloria went through some of her books, making piles of which ones she wanted to keep, and which she would donate. She clapped in delight at the new books Lou brought with her, and looked just as thrilled when Noah produced a finished dish.

Actually, Lou didn't quite get to savor the expression on

Gloria's face because her phone began ringing just as Noah began plating the dish.

"Willow, hey," Lou answered.

"Any chance you can come by the station?" Willow sounded tired, but there was an added quality to her voice, one Lou couldn't quite place.

Glancing up at Noah to stop him from scooping more than one serving, Lou said, "Yes, of course. We'll be right there."

They hung up, and Lou was met with questioning glances from both Gloria and Noah.

"Willow needs us," she said to Noah, then turned to Gloria. "I'm so sorry, but we have to go a little earlier than expected. It's my friend."

Gloria waved her hands toward Lou. "No apologies needed. Go. Go be with your friend. You two have done so much already. I can put these leftovers away." She opened her arms and walked toward Lou, enveloping her in a tight hug. "Thank you."

Making sure Noah had his list, and Lou had the clues from Fitz, the two raced out of Gloria's place, driving to the Button police station. When they arrived, Willow was slumped in one of the chairs positioned along the wall.

"Hey, what's going on?" Lou asked, racing forward. She realized she should've asked some follow-up questions earlier when she had Willow on the phone, since the possible scenarios running through her mind were turning scary as she approached her best friend.

Willow stood. "It's Quincy. They arrested him. He's one of the Muscle Car Mafia." Her tone was soft, unbelieving.

And even though Lou had filled Noah in on the possibility of Quincy being the person in the car they'd seen drive down the old access road the night before, he remained shocked that it had turned out to be the truth. Lou couldn't quite believe it either, if she were being honest.

"Oh, Willow. I'm so sorry. I know you really enjoyed having him as an employee." Lou patted her friend on the shoulder and motioned for her to take a seat again. She dragged herself like she was absolutely running on fumes.

"No, this is great news. I mean, it's creepy that he was trying to get close to me, but now we have one more person out of the running in this horrible race to hurt Easton." Willow's eyes locked on to Lou. "And apparently, I have you to thank for this."

Lou held her head at a slight angle. "George cracked the case. She was the one who saw the note sitting in your purse and figured out that only Quincy could have seen it."

"I'll have to thank her as well." Willow thrust out a breath. "Easton and the chief are interrogating him right now. I wanted you to be here when they're done, in case Easton has questions for you."

Lou and Noah dragged over chairs and made a circle so they could see one another better as they talked. They filled Willow in on Gloria and the clues they'd learned from her, as well as her newfound lease on life.

Noah's focus moved to Willow, to the crumpled, near-deflated state of the usually confident, unbreakable woman. "How's OC?"

Her mouth twitched upward, an attempt at a smile. "I think he's going to be fine," she said, the statement encased in an exhale. "But..."

"You won't know for sure for another twenty-four hours or so," Noah finished the hanging statement, knowing that even though OC had gotten through the worst of the colic symptoms last night, he could still relapse at any time.

For Willow to be here, away from him, was a big deal. As if reminded of that fact, she let her head drop forward, covering her face with her hands. "I thought moving him was going to keep him safe, not stress him out so much that he came down with colic." Tears spilled down her cheeks.

Noah set a hand on Willow's shoulder. "I know. Everyone knows how much you care about him. You moved him and Steve to keep them safe. Animals are sensitive creatures, and they don't always understand what's going on, even if it's in their best interest. I'm so sorry."

Willow gave him a small, grateful smile. But before she could say anything in response, Easton walked out of the back hallway and into the lobby. Willow got to her feet, and Lou stepped next to Noah, threading her arm through his.

Easton must've noticed the red rimming Willow's eyes, and the fresh tears streaming down her cheeks because he folded her into a tight hug. Her shoulders rose and lowered in a sigh.

Once she stepped back from him, Easton ran a hand over his face. "Well, he's talking."

Noah let out a humorless laugh. "Why doesn't that sound promising?"

"He doesn't know much," Easton said. "Apparently, the whole masked-identity bit wasn't just a ruse from Grimes to keep you two in the dark. It's actually how the group operated in the few instances when they all got together."

"What purpose would it serve to keep their identities secret?" Lou asked.

"Maybe he wanted the criminals to feel safe." Willow snorted at the irony behind that statement. "Like, no one was going to come after them in their real lives because of their involvement in the Muscle Car Mafia."

"Except Chevelle," Noah said. "And if you ask me, he's the scariest out of the bunch."

Easton agreed. "And Quincy mentioned that Chevelle had a rule that they couldn't pair up for jobs. If they needed a second, they used him. Quincy thought it was probably because two of the crew members knew each other outside the group and he didn't want them getting any ideas about cutting him out."

"So he's paranoid," Willow snorted. Sobering quickly, she added, "Did Quincy say what he was going to do to me in order to get to you?"

At that, Easton's expression darkened. "He swears he wasn't going to hurt you. He just wanted to gain your trust and see if it opened any doors to make it easier to get to me. Apparently, he doesn't usually have a plan going in, but if he spends enough time, an opening usually presents itself."

"He swears?" Willow coughed. "The word of a killer doesn't mean much to me." Though her words were supposed to be unfeeling, the way they cracked showed how much emotion still sat behind them.

"He didn't kill Cobra," Easton said. "He has a second job, at a warehouse out in Kirk. He works with two other people who said he was there the whole evening."

But Willow's trust had been shattered at that point. Hearing that the man didn't have plans to kill her, and that he hadn't killed the man they'd found in their barn, did nothing to detract from the reality that he was planning on hurting Easton.

"What does that do for your logic puzzle, Lou?" Willow

asked, changing the subject, as if she knew she wasn't doing a very good job of hiding her true feelings about the employee she'd seen as a friend.

Slipping the folded puzzle from her purse, Lou laid it out on the reception desk and borrowed a pen to mark down the information about Quincy Thatcher.

	Cobra	Mustang	Daytona	Viper	GTO	Firebird	Hotwire	Hack	Charm	Infiltrate	Violence	Pickpocket
Tyson Krate	O	X	X	X	X	X	X	X	X	X	X	O
Bex Mason	X	O	X	X	X	X	O	X	X	X	X	X
Fitz Grimes	X	X	X	X	O	X	X	X	X	X	O	X
Quincy Thatcher	X	X			X		X	X	X	O	X	X
	X	X			X		X			X	X	X
	X	X			X		X			X	X	X
Hotwire	X	O	X	X	X	X						
Hack	X	X			X							
Charm	X	X			X							
Infiltrate	X	X			X							
Violence	X	X	X	X	O	X						
Pickpocket	O	X	X	X	X	X						

After recording that he was the infiltrator, Lou turned to Easton.

"Did he tell you what his nickname is, at least?" she asked.

Easton's eyes widened. "He did. He's Daytona."

Lou squinted one eye.

ERYN SCOTT

"If you're trying to figure out what kind of tattoo that means he had, you can give yourself a break." Easton stretched out his shoulders. "He also said he's the only one on the crew who didn't get a tattoo."

	Cobra	Mustang	Daytona	Viper	GTO	Firebird	Hotwire	Hack	Charm	Infiltrate	Violence	Pickpocket
Tyson Krate	O	X	X	X	X	X	X	X	X	X	X	O
Bex Mason	X	O	X	X	X	X	O	X	X	X	X	X
Fitz Grimes	X	X	X	X	O	X	X	X	X	X	O	X
Quincy Thatcher	X	X	O	X	X	X	X	X	X	O	X	X
	X	X	X		X		X			X	X	X
	X	X	X		X		X			X	X	X
Hotwire	X	O	X	X	X	X						
Hack	X	X	X		X							
Charm	X	X	X		X							
Infiltrate	X	X	O	X	X	X						
Violence	X	X	X	X	O	X						
Pickpocket	O	X	X	X	X	X						

Poring over the puzzle in front of her, Lou said, "That still leaves us with Firebird and Viper as complete mysteries. Well, except that we know one of them was the hacker, and the other charmed victims into letting down their guard so they could steal the cars. Oh, I almost forgot." Lou slid the note from her pocket and handed it to the detective. "I got two more clues from Grimes."

"The hot-wirer can't be the colorblind one," Easton read aloud. "That makes sense. And I guess we already know that was true since we know Quincy is the one who's colorblind, and he's the infiltrator, not the hot-wirer."

Lou made the changes to the puzzle and then waited as he read the next clue.

"This sounds like it's telling us that the hacker is the one with asthma." Easton scratched at his chin.

"I thought the same thing too," Lou agreed, marking that on her puzzle.

"So, we know how everyone stole cars except for Viper and Firebird, one of whom is a hacker with asthma." Lou scrutinized the puzzle. "I think I'm going to try to make a new puzzle tonight, using the weaknesses instead of their names in this first section. Maybe that will help me see something new. Gloria said Fitz calls her every day at five, so I'll go again tomorrow night to see what other clues he's sent along."

Willow clicked her tongue and turned toward Easton. "What are you going to do with Quincy?"

Easton inhaled. "Well, since it was only conspiracy to commit murder at this point, and he's being cooperative, the chief's letting him go with a warning. But he's putting a patrol on him until the parole hearing just in case."

Lou nodded. That was yet another potential murderer off the list of whom they had to worry about. Only two remained. Easton just had to make it through this week. Why did five days suddenly feel like an eternity?

CHAPTER 18

That Monday promised to be both cozy and quiet in the bookshop. Given the slower nature of the day, Lou decided it was time to try letting NF out once more. He'd hissed less each time she'd gone in to give him fresh food and water over the weekend, and he no longer appeared to be plotting her murder while she was cleaning his litter box.

She'd also finally decided on a name for him, which made him feel like a more permanent member of the bookshop. It had been Gloria's love of Jane Austen that had spurred the idea, shaped by Lou's commitment to her belief that the new cat wasn't bad, just merely misunderstood. When she'd heard Gloria admit to naming her son Fitzwilliam, after Mr. Darcy, it had all clicked together.

"Would any of you mind if I let Fitzwilliam Clawrcy try being out and about again?" Lou asked the group of her regulars once they'd all assembled that morning.

"Clawrcy." George chuckled. "I love it."

"Classic misunderstood character," Forrest said with a nod of approval.

Silas mumbled something about not wanting to get scratched, and made his excuses to leave early, but Forrest, George, and Cricket were all game to give the grumpy cat another shot.

He slunk from the office, a low growl leaking from him the whole way as he moved through the space, settling in the corner by the used books. Clawrcy hunched into a tense loaf and crouched there for the morning, glaring at them, hissing every once in a while, but never coming toward anyone.

Lou scratched her cheek. "I'll just have to warn customers not to try to get close to him, but he doesn't seem to be a danger."

"Yeah," George said. "Nothing against Catnip, but she's kinda the same. I mean, she doesn't hiss, but she hides most of the day too."

Cricket grinned. "Agreed. Let the grump be grumpy. Who knows? Maybe he'll soften up once he spends more time around us."

Lou's heart warmed at her regulars' acceptance of him, and she went about her business as they filed off to start their days. She was dusting the shop in a lull between customers when a motion near the front door caught her eye. Turning, she observed six of the cats—even Mr. Clawrcy—crowded around the door.

This was strange, for two reasons. The first being that they all knew to give doors a wide berth, especially the front door, as it often opened throughout the day and let customers inside. Meatball had made the mistake of lying there to sun herself one morning, and Forrest had almost stepped on her when he strode inside. The second reason this gathering of cats was strange was because they were all equally drawn to the thing outside. Even when one of them was chasing a bug or following a bird perched outside the window, such activities would draw one, maybe two, other cats.

Whatever had caught their attention outside must be big.

Curious, Lou set down the duster and went over to join the felines. She bobbed her head as she peered through the panes of glass that made up the front door to the bookshop.

There, sitting just outside, was a calico cat.

It watched the long, yellow catkins hanging from the hazelnut trees as if they were the most interesting things it had ever seen. To be fair, the catkins looked an awful lot like cat toys, Lou realized. She laughed at the inquisitive way the cat watched the trees.

Then, the cat's attention moved to Lou. Its head moved from one side to the next as it considered Lou, but didn't flee as she would expect most cats to do. It also wasn't particularly dirty, as it should've been if it had been living outdoors for a while. In fact, the cat's short hair was primarily what had Lou opening the door to the bookshop and stepping out to greet it —it was far too cold for the thing to be hanging out in the freezing February temperatures.

The bookshop cats may have momentarily forgotten their wariness of the front door, but the moment the bell rang when Lou opened it, they scattered, moving to the windows on either side to continue their inspection of the new cat. Lou studied the feline after pulling the door shut behind her. It stood. Lou froze. But instead of racing away from her, the cat stretched and walked forward, rubbing against her shins.

"Well, aren't you a lovely surprise, and a bit of a mystery." Lou knelt next to the cat, holding out her hand.

Without even starting with the typical exploratory sniff, the cat launched its body forward, rubbing its face and neck on Lou's outstretched hand. When Lou reached down to test out how it would feel being picked up, the cat jumped into her arms.

Chuckling, Lou said, "Okay. It looks like you're coming inside with me. Let's give Noah a call and see if he has time to check you out."

The other cats crowded around her feet as she walked through the shop. It was a good thing Clawrcy wasn't occupying the office anymore since she didn't know if this cat had fleas or was in poor health, and didn't want to expose the other cats.

Once the new cat was safely contained, Lou texted Noah the news. He'd already been planning on coming over after picking up Marigold from school. Goldie had been excited to hear about Gloria's many cats and had asked to come with them that evening when they visited the older woman again. Noah responded that he and Goldie would be happy to come meet the newest member of the Whiskers and Words family first.

So, when Noah and Marigold showed up that afternoon, he held a bag of exam supplies at his side. Marigold rushed forward to give Lou a hug. With everything going on, it had been far too long since Lou had seen the girl, and she squeezed her extra tight to make up for it.

"We'll just be a minute while your dad checks on this new cat. Don't forget to pack a brush for when we go to Gloria's," she reminded Marigold, who nodded before drifting over to the used book section where Mr. Clawrcy sat. "And careful around him. He's a spicy one."

Marigold kept her distance, watching the new cat from across the room while Lou led Noah to the office.

HALF AN HOUR LATER, Noah had concluded that the cat was a female, was flea free, and had a microchip. He tapped his foot as he rang the number associated with the chip. He held the phone in front of him, putting the call on speakerphone so Lou could hear as well.

"Hello?" a woman's voice spilled from the speaker.

"Hi. I'm calling because we've found your cat," Noah said.

The woman cleared her throat. "Cat?"

Noah checked the website where he'd pulled up the registration information for the chip. "This is the number associated with the microchip of a calico cat. Female. About three years old. I'm Dr. Noah Ramero, a veterinarian in Button. Your cat walked up to a local bookstore today, and we're holding her here." He waited.

"Oh, Mom," the woman groused, causing Lou and Noah to share a confused look. "I'm sorry, yes. I think it was my mother's cat. This is her phone. She just passed away this weekend and..." The woman's voice wobbled until it was obvious she couldn't continue that statement.

Lou gulped at the news.

Gathering her composure, the woman continued on with her explanation. "She promised she wouldn't get any more cats, and even though we found a litter box and food inside, we thought it was left over from her last cat since we didn't see anything inside the house."

The poor thing must've been outside when her owner passed and hadn't been able to get back in. That was why she came searching for another place to stay.

"I'm so sorry for your loss," Noah said. "Is her house near Thread Lane? We can come drop the cat off with you right now, if you're there."

There was a long pause, and then an even longer sigh. "Look, the thing is … my mom was the cat person. Growing up, we always had at least six strays staying in and around our house. I hated those cats. Grew to despise them. And when I moved out on my own, I told myself I'd never have to live with another cat. So, you see, I can't take it."

Lou's eyebrows pinched together at the woman's admission. A deep furrow cut across Noah's forehead as he trained his eyes on Lou. She quickly realized he was asking her permission. Lou nodded in response, understanding the question.

"We can keep her here, if you're sure no one in the family will want her." Noah scratched the cat's ears.

"Would you? That would be amazing." Any tension in the woman's voice eased. "We've just got so much on our plates with the funeral and this house. Trying to find a home for her cat was going to be pretty far down on my list."

Even though Lou didn't understand someone not loving cats, she respected the woman's honesty and was glad the cat had found a safe place at Whiskers and Words.

"No problem," Noah said. "Sorry to bother you during this difficult time. I hope you have a good rest of your day."

He ended the call and glanced from the cat to Lou. "What are you going to call this one?" Noah asked.

Lou wet her lips. "Isn't it obvious? If the other new cat is Fitzwilliam Clawrcy, she has to be Jane Pawsten."

CHAPTER 19

Because they were already running late, Lou left Jane Pawsten in the office while they went to Gloria's. They could work on introducing her to the other cats once they returned that evening.

Noah and Lou found Marigold lying on her stomach on the love seat in the bookshop. She had a book propped on a pillow in front of her and three cats lying on her back and legs. Anne Mice had settled in a perfect loaf on the girl's shoulders. Meatball perched on Marigold's lower back, rigid to the point that she almost looked like she was being forced to be there, even though Lou knew better. And Charles Lickens was sprawled over Marigold's legs.

Sapphire, as usual, was fast asleep on a stack of books on the table near the front of the shop. And Fitzwilliam Clawrcy was curled up on a cat bed near the science fiction section, glaring at the group of cats and the girl.

Noah snapped a picture and whispered, "I think this photo would be titled Marigold's Dream."

Lou couldn't help but break into laughter at the sight. The

sound scared off Meatball, but the other two cats just blinked sleepily at her. Marigold craned her neck around, the biggest grin taking over her face.

"I hate to break up the cuddle session, Goldie, but it's time for us to go." Noah's eyes softened as he closed the distance and scooped Anne Mice from his daughter's back so she could wriggle her legs out from under Charles.

Marigold returned the book she'd been reading to the used book section and then grabbed a cat brush to show that she was ready. "Is the new cat staying?" she asked as they walked out the door.

"She is." Lou wrapped an arm around Marigold's shoulders and tugged her into her side. "And her name is Jane Pawsten."

Marigold's hazel eyes sparkled with laughter, so like her father. They climbed into Noah's truck. As they traveled to Button Lake, Lou wondered if they should warn Marigold about the state of Gloria's home, but she figured she'd leave the decision to Noah. He'd been inside the house, and he knew his daughter. If he didn't feel the need to warn the girl, Lou wouldn't worry.

Gloria was waiting for them at the open front door when they parked and walked up the overgrown path to her porch. "And who do we have here?" she asked a little gruffly, her scratchy voice tentative as she eyed the child.

"Hi, Miss Gloria. I'm Marigold Ramero." Marigold stepped forward, holding her hand out toward the older woman.

Lou's heart melted, a sentiment that both Noah and Gloria seemed to share. Gloria's features softened, and she shook the girl's hand.

"I hear you love cats. So do I." Marigold pulled the cat

brush from her pocket once Gloria had let go of her hand. "I brush the cats at Lou's bookshop a lot and wondered if yours would like to be brushed too."

Gloria blinked. "Well, you can certainly try, young lady." She stepped aside to let the group into her home.

Because Gloria still had plenty of food from their visit yesterday, they concentrated on repairs and clutter that evening. Lou brought flattened boxes from the bookshop and loaded up the books Gloria wanted to donate, as well as starting another box for other items she wanted to get out of the house.

Just before they left, Gloria slipped Lou a note from Grimes. Because Marigold was with them, Lou waited until Noah dropped her off and she was home alone to read it. Before she did so, Lou let Jane Pawsten out of the back office, giving her time to greet the rest of the cats.

She did great, as did everyone else. Fitzwilliam Clawrcy stayed put in his position in the science fiction section, but Lou counted it as a win that he didn't hiss or growl at her. She monitored the cats as she took the note from Grimes out of her pocket.

Vanity might not seem like a very tangible weakness, but this person was of the opinion that wearing glasses would take away their charm even though they desperately needed them.

Instead of taking out her puzzle, Lou pulled a fresh piece of paper from the notebook she kept by her checkout computer and drew a new grid. On this one, she wrote in all the same information, only she included the weaknesses Fitz had given her in the section instead of their real names. After she'd gone through and marked all the clues from him, she surveyed her new puzzle.

	Cobra	Mustang	Daytona	Viper	GTO	Firebird	Hotwire	Hack	Charm	Infiltrate	Violence	Pickpocket
Vain	X	X	X		X		X	X	O	X	X	X
Asthma			X		X				X	X	X	
Colorblind	X	X	O	X	X	X	X	X	X	O	X	X
Dyslexic	X	X	X	X	O	X	X	X	X	X	O	X
Perfectionist			X		X				X	X	X	
Bad knee			X		X				X	X	X	
Hotwire	X	O	X	X	X	X						
Hack	X	X	X		X							
Charm	X	X	X		X							
Infiltrate	X	X	O	X	X	X						
Violence	X	X	X	X	O	X						
Pickpocket	O	X	X	X	X	X						

Fitz had told her he was dyslexic. Quincy, or Daytona, was colorblind. The hot-wirer couldn't be the one who was colorblind, which made sense since they knew the hot-wirer had been Mustang, not Daytona. The charmer was vain, which meant that Viper or Firebird had to be vain since everyone else had already been assigned a stealing technique. Beyond that, Lou couldn't fill out anything more.

She scanned what she had left. Firebird and Viper remained the final mysteries. One was the hacker and the other the charmer. Another clue or two and she would have everything figured out.

Lou realized that once she did, she technically wouldn't need to go back to Gloria's anymore. But as quickly as the thought came, Lou swept it away. Helping Gloria hadn't been about the clues since that first meeting. It didn't matter if Fitz ran out of information to give Lou. She would continue to check on Gloria as long as the woman needed help.

That settled in her heart, Lou called for the cats to follow her upstairs. She picked up Sapphire, knowing the deaf cat wouldn't hear her like the rest of the cats, and carried him with her. As she passed by the science fiction section, she was surprised to see Clawrcy stand and stretch, following behind the group of cats as they moved toward the staircase that would bring them upstairs.

Jane Pawsten, while a little disoriented and unsure about where they were going, followed the rest of the cats as they waited at the staircase door. Lou unlocked it and headed upstairs, the small herd of felines rushing in front of her.

When she reached the apartment, Lou found Willow in the kitchen making dinner.

"Hey," Lou said, the word resembling a bit of a yelp as she jumped in surprise. She hadn't expected anyone to be there. "You're back from the farm?"

Willow nodded, knowing what Lou was really asking. "Yep. OC is steady. The vet came by again today and did a checkup. She said he's officially out of trouble."

The weight that statement took off Lou's shoulders must've

been insignificant compared to how it had felt for Willow, but it made Lou's day that much better all the same.

"Peggy ran the nursery today so I could be there with OC for his appointment, but I'm thinking I'll be able to get back to my normal schedule tomorrow." Willow stirred whatever she had sautéing on the stove.

The tightness in her tone reminded Lou that it wouldn't be completely normal. Quincy wouldn't be there. Lou was about to ask Willow how she was feeling about the whole Quincy situation when Willow's eyes caught on the new cat.

"Who's this?" Willow lowered the temperature on the burner, set down the spatula, and squatted to greet Jane Pawsten.

Lou explained the whole situation about how the cat had arrived, how her owner had passed, and finally how Lou was going to keep her at Whiskers and Words.

Willow's gaze snapped to Mr. Clawrcy as he slunk to the other side of the room. "And you're letting that guy loose?" she asked with much less warmth.

"Don't be like Silas," Lou scoffed. "He's fine. Mr. Clawrcy isn't a bad feline, he's just misunderstood."

Willow laughed at his name. "Okay, I'll give him a second chance. He sure is interested in Jane." She gestured to how the big male cat was following the calico as she investigated the apartment. "They're both fixed, right?"

Lou nodded and set Sapphire down on the couch. "Jane Austen was the creator of Mr. Darcy, so he must know they're connected." She giggled, then washed her hands so she could help with dinner.

As they cooked, they chatted about the case, and Lou filled Willow in on the newest clue she'd received from Fitz.

Hesitating in the middle of chopping vegetables, Willow asked, "You don't think the two who are left are people we've already encountered, like the others?"

Lou considered that. It *had* been the case with two of the four other members they knew about. "Cobra tried to rent Easton's house. Daytona got a job with you." Lou tapped her fingers against the kitchen counter. "Do you know anyone who fits what we know about Firebird or Viper? Anyone who's come into your life, or Easton's life, recently? A hacker or someone who's exceptionally charming?"

They laughed and thought about this as they finished cooking and as they ate. But they'd still come up empty-handed by the time they started on dishes.

Then the cats quickly took over their focus, because Mr. Clawrcy had become bolder in his trailing of Jane Pawsten. In fact, he was walking next to her, everywhere she went in the apartment. The sour cat was purring up a storm as he kept in step with the newcomer.

"It looks like I might've named her incorrectly." Lou chuckled.

"How could you get better than Jane Pawsten?"

"Well, technically, I can't because there isn't a punny version of Elizabeth Bennett. But Clawrcy sure does seem to have been bewitched by her, body and soul."

Willow laughed. "You're not wrong there. That cat is definitely in love."

As if to prove her point, Clawrcy leaned into Jane, rubbing his head against her in a display of affection Lou would've thought him incapable of just yesterday. Between Clawrcy and Gloria, Lou was rather enjoying seeing evidence that people—

and animals—could always flourish if someone just gave them a chance.

CHAPTER 20

Tuesday morning in the bookshop, Lou's regulars were astonished by the change in Clawrcy. Well, almost all her regulars. Silas didn't show.

Lou wasn't sure if he had something else to do that morning, or if he was staying away because he really was worried about getting attacked by the "bad feline."

But Lou didn't have time to dwell on those thoughts because after the regulars had gushed about Jane Pawsten, and the change in Mr. Clawrcy, George made a statement that stopped Lou in her tracks as she was putting out the new releases for the week.

"Oh, that guy I went on a date with yesterday said he really liked this author." George plucked one of the new releases from the display and casually read the back cover.

Lou's gaze flicked to Forrest and then to Cricket as they both froze, turning their attention to George as if they might not have heard her correctly. It was then that Lou remembered she and Willow had encouraged George to try dating again.

She'd found that guy who sounded promising on her app and had mentioned asking him out.

But then they'd gone through their preparations for their misinformation trap, OC had gotten sick, and Lou had started going to Gloria's in the evenings. Between it all, Lou had forgotten about her friend's dating prospects.

Being mindful to not come off as overzealous, Lou said, "Right. How'd that date go?"

George glanced up from the book. "It was good." She opened to the front page and began reading.

Good? That was … vague. George was one of the most open people Lou had ever met. Between her facial expressions, body language, and her candidness, Lou rarely had to guess what the young woman was feeling.

Studying her now, Lou felt as though she was staring at one of the books they'd wrapped in paper for the blind date display—*before* they wrote the adjectives and tropes on the front.

Was George happy about the date? Was good … good? Or did she wish it had been better? Lou couldn't tell.

She made sure George was still concentrating on the book as she looked at Cricket and Forrest. The other regulars appeared to be in shock as well. Forrest's forehead was knotted in wrinkles, and Cricket's mouth hung open in surprise.

Lou cleared her throat. "Are you going to see him again?"

"Probably." George finally set down the book. "Just not tonight or tomorrow."

Lou squinted her eyes in question.

"Because it's too close to Valentine's Day," George said slowly, motioning to the bookshop's many decorations, like she was disappointed in Lou for forgetting about the holiday. "It's too much pressure for a second date."

"That makes sense," Cricket chimed in, though her statement was far too loud.

Forrest and Lou shot warning glares in her direction.

"What was his name?" Forrest asked. "What was he like?"

"Jason." George picked up another new release and studied it as she said, "He was nice. Good looking. Kind, I think. He was nice to the server at the restaurant, at least, so I'd say that's a good start."

"Where did you go?" Cricket asked, recovering well, and joining the conversation at a more normal volume.

"The bistro." George jerked her head toward the local restaurant. "He lives in Silver Lake, but he said he's always liked Button more, so we met here."

Lou pressed her lips forward, impressed and surprised. Most of the people who lived in Silver Lake thought their city was superior to Button—sort of in the way most Buttonites felt that their sewing-themed town was a much better option to the pickle-themed town of Brine next door.

Lou smiled. "Okay, Jason from Silver Lake. This sounds like a good start."

"It definitely does." George put down the book she was looking at. "Well, I've got an appointment showing up in a few for a new laptop, so I'd better get home."

And with that, George disappeared out the door with a wave.

Cricket waited all of three seconds before she said, "That was weird. Right?"

Forrest puffed out his cheeks.

"I mean, she seemed happy?" Lou couldn't help but let her

tone lilt up at the end, turning something that should've been a statement into a question.

Forrest chuckled. "I'm glad I'm not the only one who was confused by that interaction. I definitely would've expected more gushing and description if it had actually been good."

"Yes." Cricket snorted. "The girl went on for close to half an hour the other day about how infuriating she finds Wesley's hair. But she says two sentences about Jason. He's nice?" Cricket sniffed. "No. Mark my words. There's something not right there."

It wasn't as if anyone was saying anything disparaging against George, but Lou had the sudden need to come to her friend's aid. "I don't know. Maybe he really is just a nice guy. Maybe they just had an uneventful first date. George mentioned she wanted something normal, someone who didn't drive her to frustration and leave her constantly wondering how he felt. Josh could be that for her."

Cricket and Forrest stared at Lou for a moment before Cricket burst into laughter.

"It's Jason. Not Josh." Cricket cackled. "He's so boring, you forgot his name in the middle of what you were saying in defense of him."

Even the normally stoic Forrest let a small grin sneak past his reserved expression. That insignificant gesture had more of an effect on Lou than Cricket's guffawing, and she couldn't help but join in on the laughter.

"Okay, you might have a point." Lou swiped a finger under her eyes to get rid of happy tears a moment later. "George can't like this guy if she speaks about him like that."

Forrest sighed. "I was really hoping she could move on."

"You never know." Cricket tipped up one shoulder.

"Tomorrow's Valentine's Day. Maybe love will be in the air for our young friend."

CRICKET'S PREDICTION turned out to be partly true. Love was definitely in the air the following day.

Whether George was feeling any of it, though, Lou hadn't a clue since she, and all the other regulars, stayed away from the bookshop that day. They didn't mind when it got busy, but the Valentine's Day traffic was something only rivaled by Christmas shopping.

The customers were full of love for books, for Lou's holiday-themed displays, and especially for the cats. Jane Pawsten and Mr. Clawrcy were of particular interest to the love-obsessed shoppers. They couldn't help but swoon at the way the cats cleaned one another and slept curled up together, especially given the similar theme to their punny literary names.

As much as she tried to get into the spirit, Lou couldn't. Even though she'd decorated the bookshop to prepare for the holiday a full week before, she had the distinct feeling that the holiday had snuck up on her.

Willow had confessed that she felt similarly when they'd chatted over coffee before work. They both knew they were in for crazy busy days, and used the time as a proverbial calm before the storm.

Button didn't have a florist, and while the locals had gotten used to driving to Silver Lake for their flower needs, they were excited to have the nursery in town to help with gift giving. Because what was better than a bouquet of roses? A rosebush you could plant in the ground and enjoy for years instead of days. It was a marketing idea Willow had come up with, and one she'd spent the past month advertising around town and spreading through word of mouth.

She'd hyped up the idea so much that she was quite sure the response was going to be overwhelming. And now, she would be responsible for running the nursery on her own.

"Peggy Lee and Beau can't help?" Lou had asked.

Willow swung her head back and forth definitively. "They offered, but they're also watching over OC for me. Well, Peggy Lee is," Willow added. "And while Beau can handle filling in on a regular shift, I wouldn't want to put him through the busy Valentine's Day crowds."

The hulking young man was quiet at the best of times, but when he was surrounded by people he didn't know, he shut down even further.

Willow waved a hand. "I'll figure it out."

"I would come help you, but it's going to be wild here too." Lou wrinkled her nose, as if the idea of crowded businesses was at all a bad thing. "What do you and Easton have planned tonight?" Lou asked, quickly adding, "If you have plans. I'm not saying you have to."

She knew some couples didn't celebrate the holiday.

But Willow smiled. "We normally would've stayed in and watched a movie with pizza, or something else equally cozy, but Easton figured being out in public might be better … safer." Her voice broke over the added word. She frowned, but quickly fixed it back into a grin. "So, we've got reservations at the bistro. What about you and Noah?"

"We're staying in. So we don't overlap, I'm in charge of

dinner and drinks, while Noah's taking care of appetizers and dessert."

"Sounds perfect." Willow scrunched her shoulders up close to her ears.

Lou knew it would be. After closing the shop, she went to the store to grab the ingredients for the dinner she was making. She wanted to try out a salmon Wellington and felt like this would be just the night to test it out. Everything was perfect, including the white wine she'd picked up to go with the fish, which had chilled to perfection by the time Noah arrived.

His eyes lit up at the sight of their dinner, but most of all, when they landed on Lou. Because they were staying in, she'd kept things casual with jeans and a light-pink sweater. After her busy day in the shop, she'd been tempted to throw her hair up into a messy bun, but she'd spent a few extra minutes curling it and letting it fall over her shoulders in loose waves.

"Happy Valentine's Day," Noah said, setting down the dishes he carried and wrapping her in his arms. His hands were immediately in her hair, confirming that she'd made the right choice in taking the time to style it. "You look beautiful, as always."

Lou kissed him. "Happy Valentine's Day," she repeated as she finally stepped back.

Suddenly Noah wasn't the only one staring in appreciation at his significant other; she couldn't help but ogle the man, just a little. He looked even more delicious than the chocolate dessert he'd set on the counter. The heather-gray cashmere sweater he wore fit him perfectly and made Lou want to curl up against him. Worried they might get sidetracked, Lou turned their attention to the food.

"What did you bring?"

Pride shone in Noah's expression as he unveiled the appetizer. "I made some bacon-wrapped dates to start," he said as he took the lid off a long glass dish. "And we have a flourless chocolate torte for dessert." He motioned toward the luxuriously dark cake Lou had already noticed. "What did you make?"

"Salmon Wellington and braised leeks, paired with white wine."

Noah beamed. "The bistro's got nothing on the two of us together."

Before Lou could agree, Noah's phone rang. He pulled it out of his pocket and frowned at the screen.

"Sorry, I've got to take this. It's a client." His eyes held an extra apology as he glanced up at Lou, but she waved off his worries. "Rylie, how's she doing?" There was a tense silence as Noah listened. "You're sure?" He ran a hand over his face. "Okay, yes. I'll meet you at the clinic." His eyes held on to Lou as he talked, the apology deepening as it became clear that one of his clients needed emergency help.

Once Noah's call was finished, he regarded their dinner.

"Lou, I'm so sorry. Rylie's cat is in labor. There are a few markers in Duchess's pregnancy that have me a little concerned, so I told Rylie I wanted to monitor the birth. I didn't think it would happen on Valentine's Day."

"It's completely fine, Noah. Duchess can't help that she went into labor." Lou paused. "Um, how long does cat labor take?"

"It could take all night." Noah winced.

Chewing on her lip for a moment, Lou surveyed the spread on the table. "You know what? I'd bet I can pack this up and bring it to you at the clinic. It's going to be a lot of waiting and monitoring, right? You'll be able to eat?"

Noah nodded carefully. "Are you sure? Having a romantic dinner here is a lot different from eating at the table in the staff room of the clinic." He chuckled.

"Of course. Plus, I've never seen a cat give birth. It'll be interesting."

Noah rushed forward, placing his hands on either side of her face as he planted a kiss on her lips. "Thank you. I love you. I'll see you there."

He slid on his boots and clomped down the stairs as she took containers out of her cabinets to transport the food.

CHAPTER 21

B y the time Lou arrived at the Button Veterinary Clinic, Duchess's owner had dropped her off, and Noah had the cat comfortably contained so he could monitor her. Light piano music played in the back room of the clinic.

"Just trying to make her feel as relaxed as possible," Noah whispered to Lou as he took the bag holding their containers of food from her.

Lou crept over to the enclosure, full of blankets and a very pregnant, fluffy white cat. "Good luck, Duchess," she whispered.

The cat blinked its green eyes at her, and the motion would've appeared indifferent if she wasn't also breathing hard with the beginnings of labor.

Lou left her alone, following Noah into the break room. Her heart fluttered as she took in the scene in front of her. Noah stood next to the break-room table where his vet techs and Kathleen ate their lunches. He'd covered it with a red tablecloth, and about fifteen tea lights burned where they'd been placed around the room.

"We keep these in case the power ever goes out." Noah's eyes danced in the candlelight.

Now it was Lou's turn to rush over to him and plant a kiss on his lips. "I love you."

They almost forgot about food altogether, but Noah pulled back and whispered, "I'm going to go check on Duchess. I'll be right back."

"I'll plate the food," Lou said, getting to work.

Everything was delicious. Lou couldn't stop raving about Noah's appetizer. He said the salmon Wellington she'd made was the best meal he'd had in a long time. They clinked their forks together before each slicing into their respective pieces of the chocolate torte. Between the piano music playing for Duchess and the tea lights, it was a cozy and romantic dinner.

Once the dishes had been cleared, they moved into the room where Duchess was. Noah brought in a few rolling office chairs for them. After a few iterations, they found a comfortable way to position their chairs next to each other. Lou rested her head on Noah's shoulder, and they whispered words of encouragement to the soon-to-be momma cat.

THURSDAY MORNING, Lou was dragging. Duchess had been in labor until just past midnight, and Lou hadn't gotten home and to bed until one in the morning. She'd been extra quiet coming home, knowing Willow would be fast asleep in the spare room, home hours earlier from her Valentine's dinner with Easton at the bistro.

Lou had texted Willow from the clinic to let her know where she was and that she'd likely be home late so her friend wouldn't worry. She was excited to debrief about their evenings over coffee, but Willow was already gone when she woke up. A note on Lou's counter explained Willow had gone out to the farm to visit OC and Steve for a few minutes before she had to come back and open the nursery.

So, Lou got ready alone, an odd sensation after having her friend there for the week. She and the cats headed downstairs to open the shop. She was taking down her Valentine's displays when George, Cricket, Silas, and Forrest all came bustling in at once.

"Good morning," she called, chuckling to see them all enter together.

They called out grin-laden greetings and took their usual spots around the shop.

"And how was your Valentine's Day?" Cricket asked Lou with a slight eyebrow waggle. "Did Noah spoil you?"

As Noah's mother's best friend, Cricket was an honorary aunt to the man. She thought the world of him. She'd also given the two a bit of a push together the summer prior and loved to take credit for their relationship.

"Wonderful and eventful." Lou beamed, filling her regulars in on their last-minute change in plans. "Duchess is doing well, as are her four kittens. And what about you and Peter? Did you have a good evening?" Lou asked.

Cricket adopted a sly look. "Always. We love Valentine's Day. Peter took me to that new Italian restaurant in Silver Lake. It was decadent." She shimmied her shoulders as if one of the dishes was sitting in front of her right now and she was about to dig in. "What about you and Gianna, Forrest?"

The quiet man inclined his head. "We had a night in with a bottle of wine and one of our favorite movies. Perfect."

Lou's heart felt warm, loving the different traditions of each couple.

George grunted from where she was sitting with Anne Mice in the seating area. "Looks like it's just you and me who were without romantic Valentine's Day plans, Silas," she deadpanned.

"Speak for yourself," Silas grumbled. "I had a date."

Everyone turned to blink at him in question.

"Good for you, Silas." Lou pressed her lips together to hide the grin that wanted to break free, knowing Silas would chastise her for showing too much emotion surrounding news of his love life.

"Who with?" Cricket asked.

"None of your business is who." Silas snapped his newspaper up in front of his face, bringing that conversation to an abrupt end.

Cricket, Forrest, Lou, and George exchanged quick glances of amusement.

"Speaking of love," Cricket said, changing the subject slightly, "these two are absolutely adorable." She gestured to Fitzwilliam Clawrcy and Jane Pawsten who were snuggled together, sharing a cat bed near the fireplace.

Lowering his newspaper, Silas frowned at Mr. Clawrcy. "Are you sure this is the same cat? Figures. I don't show for a couple days and everything changes around here."

The contented sounds of purring vibrated off the pair, audible halfway across the room.

Lou laughed. "Yep, that's the same cat on the outside, but he's gotten a new lease on life ever since this little lady joined us."

Her regulars left a while later, leaving Lou and the cats to their quiet Thursday. It was so slow that Lou was contemplating closing for an hour so she could pick up lunch and eat with Noah at the clinic. But before she could think further on that idea, the bell chimed on the front door. Lou looked up from where she'd been working to dismantle some of the larger Valentine's Day displays.

Wesley St. James wandered inside Whiskers and Words. "Hey, Lou." He sauntered in his usual unhurried way, but there was a tightness to his demeanor that told her something was off.

"What can I do for you, Wesley?" She noticed him staring at Mr. Clawrcy, probably wondering if the sweet cat was the same one he'd brought in just a week earlier, hissing and growling. "Come to check on your friend? As you can see, he's found his place."

Wesley scoffed. "I'd say he has. Either that or you switched him out for another cat." He strode over to the new-release table, idly scanning the titles.

Lou observed him for a moment before asking her question again. "Are you here for a book, or did you need something else?"

"I just wanted to stop by and check to see if there were any developments in the Muscle Car Mafia case. You know. For Doug."

"Oh?" Lou tapped her finger against the counter. "What did Doug want to know?"

Wesley cut the air with his palm. "Doug didn't ask anything specific. In fact, he didn't ask me to come at all. But I like to check in with him from time to time about the cases we've worked on together so that he doesn't fire me."

The glance that had passed between Wesley and Doug at the diner after Doug had mentioned his last PI came to mind.

"Is that what happened with his last PI? The one who looked into the Muscle Car Mafia for him? He didn't check in enough?"

Wesley coughed. "Oh, no. That guy was terrible. Doug fired him because he would do the bare minimum and half the time would report things that weren't true just because they were convenient." His gaze lingered on the seating area for a moment, then he craned his neck to see down one of the aisles of bookshelves. "George not here? I thought she liked to hang out during the day."

"She mostly comes in the morning." Lou's lips twitched, but she held the grin at bay. "Did you need her?"

Wesley's eyes went wide. "Need her? Psh. No. Not at all. Absolutely not." His cheeks flushed with color.

"She's probably at her place, if you want to look for her there." Lou hitched a thumb behind her, toward George's house that doubled as the Tech Emporium for the town.

"No," he answered far too quickly. "I just—well, I was going to ask you something. I saw her out with some guy on Monday night, and I was wondering if her brother was visiting." He focused on the new releases.

"George is an only child. That was a date." Lou's tone flattened, finding it silly that she even needed to say any of that aloud since it seemed clear that Wesley already knew it.

He finally looked at Lou. "Did they go out yesterday too? For Valentine's Day."

Swallowing a sigh, Lou said, "Wesley, look, George's dating life is her own business."

"Right. Sorry. I—"

"But," Lou interrupted what was sure to be a rambling apology, "I will say that, if you have feelings for her, you should tell her."

Any embarrassment in his features hardened into incredulity. "Feelings?" He spat out the question. "Oh, no. Me and George? No. We ... I was just ... This isn't..." He didn't finish any of those broken thoughts. Turning toward the door, Wesley said, "I've got a client to meet with. Sorry to run."

"Wesley." Lou's voice stopped him.

He reluctantly met her gaze.

"Not liking cats is a big deal-breaker for her. When you dropped off Mr. Clawrcy, it made her think you aren't interested in cats." Lou wanted to say more, but she left it at that.

Understanding seemed to ping in Wesley's mind, rewarding Lou for her careful word choice. In the span of a moment, his flustered attitude was gone, replaced by his usual swagger. "Mr. Clawrcy?" he asked with a smirk.

"Fitzwilliam," Lou said. "It was fitting since he's such a classically misunderstood character."

Wesley opened his mouth, but the front door swung open, stopping him.

"Gloria?" Lou blinked as the older woman tottered inside the bookshop. She was surprised to see the woman outside her home, and wouldn't have believed her eyes if Wesley hadn't also turned to see the woman enter.

Raising a hand in a wave, Wesley said, "I'll see you around, Lou. Thanks."

She couldn't let her thoughts linger too much on her encounter with Wesley—or what it might mean—because Gloria was walking farther into the bookshop, glancing around in awe. The smile already on her face grew as she took in the cats and books. Her breath came in pants, and she placed a hand on her hip as if she might have a stomach cramp.

"Did you walk here?" Lou asked, moving around the register counter so she could lead the woman over to the seating area.

Gloria panted as she followed Lou's lead and took a seat in the plushy armchair. "I did." She was still breathless.

"Are you sure that's a good idea? What about your back?"

Gloria swatted dismissively at Lou. "I need to move more. When I used to go on daily walks, my back always felt better. It hurts the most when I just sit in my chair all day." Her eyes shone with excitement. "So, this is your place. I love it."

Pride won out over worry, and Lou's mouth broke into a grin. "Thank you."

Gloria inhaled sharply. "Oh, I have something for you." She dug around in the pocket of her jacket, paper crinkling against her fingers. She proffered a folded note toward Lou a moment later. "Fitzy called last night, and I thought you'd better see this clue."

Heart jumping from a regular rhythm to a racing one in the span of a few seconds, Lou took the note from Gloria. "I'm sorry. With yesterday being Valentine's Day, I—"

"Don't you worry about it," Gloria said, stopping her from apologizing just as Lou had done to Wesley minutes earlier. She snapped her fingers toward the note.

Lou opened it. It held two clues. The first one was straight forward.

Viper always seemed so weak to me, but I

*have to admit that he scared me sometimes with
what he could do behind a keyboard.*

Okay. That seemed pretty straightforward. Viper had to be the hacker, which meant he was also the one with asthma. Lou marked that on her puzzle before moving onto the next clue.

I always knew I could beat Mustang in a foot race, given how she limped with her bad knee, but hand to hand was a different story. She was terrifying. Unhinged. If I had to face her today, I'd run.

That word rang in Lou's mind. Unhinged. Easton had used the same word when describing Fitz to her and Willow.

She pulled out her puzzle, the newest iteration with the weaknesses instead of names, marking that Mustang had the bad knee.

	Cobra	Mustang	Daytona	Viper	GTO	Firebird	Hotwire	Hack	Charm	Infiltrate	Violence	Pickpocket
Vain	X	X	X	X	X		X	X	O	X	X	X
Asthma	X	X	X	O	X	X	X	O	X	X	X	X
Colorblind	X	X	O	X	X	X	X	X	X	O	X	X
Dyslexic	X	X	X	X	O	X	X	X	X	X	O	X
Perfectionist		X	X	X	X		X	X	X	X	X	
Bad knee	X	O	X	X	X	X	O	X	X	X	X	X
Hotwire	X	O	X	X	X	X						
Hack	X	X	X	O	X	X						
Charm	X	X	X	X	X							
Infiltrate	X	X	O	X	X	X						
Violence	X	X	X	X	O	X						
Pickpocket	O	X	X	X	X	X						

Just like that, Lou saw the puzzle come together. The only weakness left for Cobra was perfectionist. If she marked that, the only weakness left for Firebird would be vanity, which also matched since the only car stealing method left for Firebird was charm. She made the last few marks.

"I finished it," Lou muttered, more to herself than Gloria.

Gloria craned her neck to see. "I don't think so, dear. You've got a mistake here."

"What?"

Gloria tapped the puzzle. "My Fitzy wasn't violent."

Lou inhaled a steadying breath. "Look, Gloria…" She didn't know how to finish that sentence. Mothers always saw the best in their kids. She probably didn't want to admit that her little boy had turned out to be so terrifying.

"Lou." Gloria's tone was tight and serious. "I'm well-aware of who my son is. I also know that he's in prison right now for assault. But that is not how he used to steal cars. His specialty was hot-wiring." She punctuated the sentence with a single nod.

But Lou didn't move. She stared at the puzzle.

"No." When Lou looked up, Gloria was scowling at her. She shook out of her fog of confusion. "Sorry, Gloria. I'm not trying to tell you that you're wrong, but how can that be true? Mustang was the hot-wirer. Bex Mason was a hot-wiring expert. Chevelle killed her after the job at Doug Cromwell's house went wrong and he was arrested."

Clearing her throat, Gloria said, "I don't know what to say about that, other than the fact that Fitz was the one who was the hot-wire expert in the group." Gloria stood, patting Lou on the shoulder. "Now, then, I've already made my way through one of those books you brought me, and I need the next in the series." Gloria wandered toward the bookshelves.

Reluctantly, Lou stood and helped Gloria find the book she needed instead of stewing in the possibility that her puzzle was filled out incorrectly. She shoved Fitz's latest clue and the puzzle into her purse as Gloria paid for the book.

"Can I drive you home?" Lou asked her as she handed over Gloria's purchase.

"Sure. It was a bit longer of a walk here than I realized."

Lou didn't mind closing early since it had been her slowest day in weeks. Together, they locked up the shop, climbed into Lou's car, and Lou drove Gloria home. Lou didn't drive directly home, however. After Gloria's, Lou drove to the police station. She was in her head so much that she didn't even stop at the front desk, simply walking straight to Easton's office. Officer Reynolds must've just let her go by because no one stopped her.

Easton glanced up from his desk as she entered. "Lou, hey." He stood, scanning her to make sure everything was okay.

She softened her features, realizing she must look pretty grim to get that reaction from Easton. "Hey, I'm wondering if you can get in contact with Quincy for me and ask him to verify something." She pulled the completed puzzle out of her purse. "I just got another clue from Fitz, and I finished the puzzle. But Gloria told me Fitz was the hot-wire expert, not the one who used violence. I just need to get the opinion of someone who's not Fitz's mother, because, of course, she thinks the best of him."

"Lou, I can't ask Quincy."

"Hmmm. Maybe we should get ahold of Doug Cromwell, then. He might know. Maybe his PI left something out. He was pretty sure Bex Mason had been a hot-wirer, but maybe he got that part wrong. Wesley mentioned that he sometimes got information wrong."

"Lou," Easton said again, more forcefully that time.

She blinked up at him, noticing that she'd been gone in that mind fog once again. "Sorry."

"I can't ask Quincy," he repeated. "I can't ask him anything because Quincy Thatcher is dead. Someone killed him this morning."

CHAPTER 22

"Dead?" An icy feeling sliced through Lou. "Killed?" She reached out for the chair next to her. Finding its position, she stepped to the right and sank into it.

Easton's throat worked through a swallow. "Same MO as Tyson's killer. Knife to the chest."

Lou's fingers curled on the puzzle in her hand, crumpling it. "I thought he had an officer watching him until the parole hearing tomorrow."

"He did. It happened during the change in shift. He was alone for five minutes, max, and that was enough time for the killer to get to him. Look," Easton said with a sigh. "This changes things."

Glancing up, Lou studied her friend.

His expression was serious. "I thought I would just need to focus on trying to stay alive through the parole hearing tomorrow, but now with two murders on our hands, I can't just sit around and hide. I have to do something. The killer left fingerprints on the knife this time so now we have something more concrete to work off of."

"What are you saying?"

"I've sent a message to Chevelle saying I'd like to meet with a representative of his this evening to talk about options for tomorrow." Easton's blue eyes were focused, decided.

"A representative of his?"

"I told him whoever he felt comfortable sending would be fine with me. It might be a lawyer, or it could be the killer. Leaving it open to him is the best way to ensure we lure the killer out of hiding. Or maybe he'll send a lawyer, and the killer will be in the background, waiting to get to me in case the negotiations don't go well." Easton shrugged. "We won't know until we meet up."

"Don't you think Chevelle will be suspicious of your sudden change of heart? He's going to know it's a trap."

There was something like fire in Easton's eyes as he said, "I'm counting on it. I want him desperate and paranoid. I want him to make a mistake. Once the parole hearing's over tomorrow, we might never hear from the killer again. This is our last chance to catch them."

Inhaling deeply, Lou said, "Well, I don't envy you telling Willow about this plan."

The reason Willow had been so on board with the last operation was because Easton wasn't actually supposed to be in any of the places they said he would. This would be entirely different.

Easton grimaced. "Yeah. It's not going to be fun."

Lou left him, stuffing her puzzle into her coat pocket and returning to the bookshop. She'd just closed for the evening when

Willow stomped into the shop via the back door. She caught sight of Lou in the bookshop and stalked forward instead of going upstairs. Her fingers curled and uncurled in and out of fists at her side as she tried to release her anxiety through the movement.

"I'm guessing Easton told you about his plan," Willow said, her words somehow managing to be blazing hot and icy cold all at once.

"He did."

Willow exhaled her frustration in a huff. "I know it's the right thing, but I'm worried about him."

Lou walked to her friend and pulled her into a hug. "Of course you are, but the entire station's going to be behind him. He'll have backup."

"He will," Willow agreed.

"Do you want to watch a movie to take your mind off everything?"

Willow thought for a moment, and then said, "As tempting as that sounds, I think I'd like to go see OC and Steve." When Lou frowned at the idea of Willow leaving her sight, she added, "Don't worry. I'll be with Peggy Lee. No one's going to mess with her."

Lou laughed, unable to argue with that. The older woman could give Gloria a run for most grumpy, especially now that the latter was in such better spirits. "Okay. But be careful."

Willow said she would and left back through the door she'd just come through. Lou took the cats upstairs and fed them dinner. She considered watching a movie, the suggestion she'd made to Willow earlier sounding cozy on a cold evening like this one. But then she thought about Gloria. It was just past five. Maybe Fitz would have one more clue for her. It could make all the difference.

Making a decision, she made sure the cats were all fed before heading out to her car. But she froze in the alley behind her bookshop. Her car wasn't the only one there.

Willow was still parked behind her.

Lou approached her friend's car. She wasn't inside, or anywhere else in the vicinity. Jogging, Lou checked the street. No Willow. She took out her phone and called, but Willow didn't pick up. Then she sent a few worried text messages.

> Hey. Where are you?

> Willow, I'm staring at your car, but you're not in it.

> Did you decide against going to the farm?

She paced for five minutes as she waited. When she still hadn't heard from Willow, and had tried calling twice more, she remembered to check her security camera. Opening the feed, she skipped the last entry, which would show her walking into the alley just minutes earlier, and picked the one that showed Willow leaving.

Clicking on the event, she waited for the video clip to begin. She held her breath as Willow pushed her way out of the bookshop's back door and walk to her vehicle. Keys in hand, Willow stopped at her car and turned toward the road. Lou's camera wasn't angled in a way that she could see what was at the end of the alley, but Willow walked toward it.

Once she was out of the frame, the video continued for another few seconds, and then it ended.

Lou's mind whirred with questions. Had Willow seen someone she knew? Did she forget something at the nursery and decide to go on foot? But why wasn't she answering her phone?

Out of options, Lou dialed Easton's number, hoping she wasn't ruining his meeting with Chevelle's representative.

"Hey, Lou," he answered right away. "I just got back to the station. No one showed at the meeting spot." His tone was flat, like it had been run over by a bus. It was obvious that his inability to meet with Chevelle's representative had put him in a foul mood.

She hated to further ruin his evening.

"Sorry to bug you, but Willow's not with you, is she?" Lou's stomach roiled with worry.

Her panic was mirrored in Easton's tone as he said, "She's not. Why?"

"She said she was going to Milton Farm to see OC and Steve, but her car is still here at the bookshop. She isn't answering my calls or texts either."

There was a muffled swear, and then Easton spoke to someone in the background, probably other officers, filling them in on the situation. The word *situation* sank to the bottom of Lou's gut.

Then Easton was back, speaking to her. "I'm sending Brenner over with Officer Peanut Butter," he said, referencing the part Bloodhound K9 officer. "I'm going home to see if she's there. I'll let you know if I find anything."

"Okay." The word was too small. She said goodbye to Easton before tears sprang into her eyes. It was becoming increasingly clear that Willow was in trouble.

Needing to busy herself, Lou texted all her friends while she waited for Officer Brenner. She sent messages to Noah, George, and Cricket to make sure Willow wasn't with them.

They all confirmed that she wasn't. She was texting Noah back, telling him to stay put until she knew more, when Brenner arrived. Peanut Butter strained at the end of his leash as he sniffed the ground the moment Brenner let him out of the cruiser.

Brenner's attention zeroed in on Willow's car. "I'm going to have Peanut Butter get her scent from her car." He said a series of commands, and the dog went to work, smelling the door handle and then following the scent in the direction Willow had walked in the video footage.

But any hope disappeared as Peanut Butter stopped at Thimble Drive. He sniffed right and then left but had obviously lost the scent.

"What about the nursery? Do you think she might've gone there?" Brenner asked, walking the dog back toward Lou.

Lou's shoulders bobbed up and then back down. The nursery was in that direction, and it was close enough that Willow could've walked. "She might've."

Brenner seemed glad to have a direction. "We'll swing by there on our way to her place so you can talk to Easton. Get in." He pointed to his cruiser, and they climbed in.

In the relative silence of Brenner's patrol car, Lou asked, "You don't think Chevelle got to her instead?"

It had always been a possibility. It was exactly why Willow had been staying with Lou in the first place, and she'd failed by letting Willow out of her sight.

Brenner sighed, unable to answer her question. He brought the car to a stop in the parking lot of Valley Nursery, telling Officer Peanut Butter they were going to do a sweep. The dog knew what that meant because the moment he was out of the car, his nose was on the ground. The nursery gates were locked, and the light in the tiny house that acted as Willow's office was off. But the group of three moved around the perimeter of the garden center, Peanut Butter sniffing while Lou called Willow's name.

Lou hated the idea of giving up. She checked her phone again to make sure Easton hadn't called with news, but her notifications were terrifyingly empty. She focused on not breaking into tears as Brenner drove them to Willow and Easton's home.

By the time they reached the house, Easton had himself in a full panic. Lou had never seen him so frustrated. His blond hair was a mess from raking his fingers through it, and his gray eyes were dark with a dangerous mixture of anger and fear.

"No luck?" His focus swept over Lou's face, searching for any scrap of hope.

She couldn't bring herself to say the words aloud, so she simply shook her head, wishing for one of Willow's signature too-tight hugs right about then.

"She has to be safe," Easton said, resuming his pacing.

"I'll drive around town and ask if anyone's seen her," Brenner offered. When Easton bowed his head in thanks, he disappeared out the front door.

Officer Reynolds stopped Easton with a hand on his shoulder. He wore an expression softer than Lou had ever seen the cranky officer sport. The moment Easton stopped and met his gaze, Reynolds said, "I think it's time to call in the chief. We need to look at this as a missing person's case. Every second counts if we want to find Willow alive."

CHAPTER 23

Easton's skin was such a pale color, he almost looked green. He raked his fingers through his hair once again.

The sight of the detective sick with worry was completely unsettling for Lou. She'd always known Easton to be in control, even in terrifying situations. But seeing him come to grips with the fact that Willow was in trouble made nausea roll over her.

"We need to get back to the station," Easton whispered.

Reynolds took out his phone. "I'll call the chief and give him a heads-up that we're on our way."

If the normally ornery officer's helpfulness surprised anyone other than Lou, no one showed it—or maybe they didn't have the capacity to focus on it at the moment.

Easton's phone buzzed with an incoming text message a moment later. Snatching it up so quickly that he almost dropped it, Easton fumbled until the screen faced him. The hope in his expression flattened.

"It's the renters," Easton said with a groan. "They think the pilot light on that old furnace may have gone out and need help relighting it."

Lou shouldn't have been surprised. They'd had terrible timing since they'd moved in. Of course they'd need something in the middle of an emergency like this.

Easton's countenance appeared almost ashen at that point, and Lou knew he didn't have the mental space or emotional energy to help them.

"Can't you tell them to do it themselves?" Irritation grated through her as she voiced the question.

"If they do it wrong, they could make everything worse." Easton pinched his eyes shut tight, as if he were trying to convince himself he was sleeping, that this was a nightmare.

Lou reached out and placed a hand on his arm, meeting his eyes when they flashed open at the touch. "I'll go. You've got to go talk to the chief. I'll help them, and then I'll meet you at the station."

"You don't have a car."

"I'll walk. It'll be good for me to get some fresh air." Lou wasn't under any illusions that she was going to be the most important person working on Willow's disappearance. The few minutes it would take her to walk from Willow's to the station wouldn't make or break the investigation.

Easton thanked her, moving to follow Reynolds out to the cars. Stepping out into the frigid evening together, Lou branched off to the left as they piled into their cruisers and backed out, driving toward the station.

She made her way through Willow and Easton's front yard, over to the rental house. The moment she set foot on the porch, the front door swung open, and a wide-eyed Rachel met her.

"Oh! You're not Easton." She squinted as if she needed to be sure.

"I'm Lou. We met the other day."

Rachel's expression softened. "Oh, right. Sorry, Lou. Is Easton coming? We texted Willow, but she's not answering." Rachel stepped back to let Lou inside.

"Easton's a little busy at the moment. Both of them are, actually. I volunteered to come help, but don't worry, I had a pilot light on my stove in my first apartment in New York City. It would go out all the time, so I know what it smells like and what to look for."

"Thank you. Micah's in the garage," Rachel said. "I love that jacket you're wearing. Very cute."

Nice as it was to get a compliment, Lou wasn't in the mood for any of this. She wanted to know what was going on with her friend.

Almost as if she could sense that Lou was thinking about Willow, Rachel said, "You and Willow must be really close if you're coming over to help with her renters."

Nodding, Lou concentrated on keeping the tears that crowded her eyes at the mention of her best friend at bay. But she didn't dare mention Willow's disappearance to Rachel. The Ashleys had been on the verge of moving out after hearing about Tyson's body being found in Willow's barn. Hearing that the trouble was rising rather than decreasing wouldn't help their peace of mind.

Rachel gestured for Lou to follow her toward the garage. Unaware of the emotional turmoil her words created in Lou, the woman continued on with the topic. "I wish I had a best friend like that. It's kind of the dream. I mean, I've got Micah, and I know it's important to have your significant other be your best friend, but there's just something about girlfriends that's special." She gave Lou a small smile.

The rawness and hope behind it made Lou temporarily feel at ease. She returned the smile as best she could and waited as Rachel led her into the garage. The garage doors were closed, but the side door was open, letting in fresh air. Even so, Lou could smell the telltale aroma of gas in the space.

On the floor of the garage, lying on his side, Micah shone a flashlight into the furnace. The access panel was propped next to him. Writhing around on the floor had caused the leg of his jeans to ruck up near his calf. Ink snaked along his ankle, moving up his leg. Snaked. It was obviously the head of a snake, and the size suggested that it spanned most of his leg.

Suddenly, all of Lou's unease returned. Was that an innocent snake tattoo? Or was that a viper, specifically? Instinctively, her hand slipped into her coat pocket where the logic puzzle sat with the clues about the Muscle Car Mafia. Her heart hammered in her throat as Micah turned to glance in their direction.

"Lou came instead," Rachel explained.

Micah clicked off the flashlight. "Oh, wonderful. Thank you for coming. Do you know anything about these machines?" he asked, standing up and dusting off his pants and shirt. "I can handle anything on a computer, but this is foreign to me."

"I do. I'd be happy to look for you." Lou congratulated herself on keeping her voice level despite the rising panic inside her as she stepped over to the furnace. Lou knelt next to the machine, pretending to search for the pilot light and the button to relight it as she thought through what she'd just seen on Micah's leg.

A hand gripped her shoulder. Lou jumped, whipping her head around to see Micah's hand there. Gaze moving up to his face, she noticed he held the flashlight out with his other hand.

"Did you want this?" he asked. "Makes it easier to see." There was a hint of teasing in the grin at the edges of his mouth.

She grabbed the flashlight and shone it into the space. Her heart calmed. Micah wasn't a member of the Muscle Car Mafia. Snakes were like horses. A lot of people had tattoos of them. That didn't make them criminals. With that worry off her mind, Lou located the pilot light. It was out.

"I found it," she called from where she crouched next to the furnace. "If you want to hand me a lighter, I can get it lit again."

"Oh, that's awesome. I wasn't even sure what I was looking for." Micah laughed. "I couldn't even really be sure it was out, but I came in here to grab something from the freezer, and I thought the air smelled funny. Then my asthma started acting up, and it wouldn't subside until I opened that side door to let in some air." He held a butane lighter with a long neck toward her.

Lou's fingers shook as she took it from him. She worked to not make eye contact with him, turning quickly back toward the furnace.

Her mind raced as she took in this latest clue. A snake tattoo might've been a coincidence, but asthma? Lou took a gulp of air, remembering that one of the two people left in the Muscle Car Mafia was the hacker, a hacker with asthma.

Micah was Viper.

Lou felt the truth of the statement in her bones. She'd inadvertently gotten herself in a room with one of the remaining people trying to kill Easton. Sheer panic crushed any sense of calm. Clicking the lighter, she held it close to the pilot light as she held the button. She needed to light this thing and get out of there. But the lighter wouldn't work. Either it was empty or her fingers were shaking too much for her to get a good click on the ignition button.

"Is that not working?" Rachel asked. "It might be out. Micah, why don't you grab the other one for her from the fireplace?"

Rachel's request reminded Lou that she wasn't alone. Micah walked back into the house, and Lou wondered if Rachel knew about her husband's past.

"Sorry about this," Rachel said. "We're good at a lot of things, but house repairs are not on that list. I can act like I know how to do most things, but this isn't one of them."

Lou's mind focused on the logic puzzle in her pocket. She reached for it, trying to remember what it said without pulling it out. If Viper was the hacker, Firebird had to be the charmer, the one who used her acting skills to make people feel at ease and flattered so they dropped their guard. What was the last weakness? Vanity. Firebird needed glasses but thought she looked better without them.

Rachel squinting at Lou at the door hadn't been about her not remembering her—she hadn't been able to see who it was.

Lou's whole body flushed hot, then cold. She froze. What if the two members of the Muscle Car Mafia, who knew each other beforehand, were acquainted because they were in a relationship?

Saturday afternoon flashed into her memory. Willow had stopped here, upset about the furniture they'd set out on the road instead of taking care of it themselves. She'd mention

Quincy. Fitz might not have known the other members' real names, but the Ashleys had seemed oddly interested in Willow's employee. Had she and Willow handed over information about Daytona's whereabouts for them, making him easier to kill?

The information felt like a keystone for the structure of suspicion she was building in her mind. This held it all together.

Rachel and Micah Ashley were Firebird and Viper.

They must've taken Willow. Lou needed to get to the police station, and fast, so she could tell Easton.

"Here we go. Try this one." Micah stepped back into the garage, holding a similar lighter with a different colored plastic base.

Lou removed her hand from her pocket and reached for the new lighter, setting the first one down next to her. She squirmed forward and tried the new lighter.

But this one had the same issue. It wasn't the lighter. Her shaking fingers couldn't seem to make the thing work.

"Sorry, I ... My fingers are stiff from the cold."

Micah knelt next to her. "Here. I can do it. Just show me where to point it," he said patiently.

She did, her finger quaking even more without the lighter to grip.

Micah pressed the button, clicked on the lighter, and a small flame transferred from the lighter to the pilot light. A paper crinkled in the background, but Lou didn't think much about it as she and Micah backed away and stood.

"Well, there you go." She shoved her hands into her pockets but noticed something was missing. The paper. The puzzle.

It must've slipped out when Lou had gone to reach for the lighter, and now … she turned to see it clutched in Rachel Ashley's hands.

Rachel's charm and Micah's tolerance disappeared as they looked over the puzzle, then at Lou. Micah's gaze dropped to her shaking hands. He knew she'd figured it out.

"Where's Willow?" Lou croaked out the question, fear skittering up and down her spine.

Micah clicked his tongue. "Oh, we can't possibly tell you that. Then what would we keep as collateral?"

Lou's mind whirred. "Collateral? You mean, she's alive?"

"Of course she is." Rachel smiled sweetly. "And she'll stay that way as long as Easton makes sure Chevelle is granted parole tomorrow. You see, Chevelle has the tendency to overreact. Killing? That's not our style, and it's also not the only way to get something done."

Micah nodded his agreement with what his wife had said. "After watching the two of them together for a month, we knew Easton would do anything for Willow. Once Chevelle is free, he'll give us the money, and we'll give Easton the location where we're keeping Willow."

"We, of course, will be long gone by then," Rachel said as she moved the puzzle closer to her so she could read it. "Psh. I am not vain."

Micah snaked an arm around her shoulder and said, "Of course you are, honey. That's why I love you." He turned his focus back to Lou. "Now, Easton really messed things up by sending you instead of coming himself. We need him here in order to explain to him what he has to do tomorrow. Do you think he'll come searching for you on his own, or will you need to text him to get him here?"

Lou's throat felt dry. She couldn't seem to answer them, her mind still going over what they'd told her.

"I told him I'd be at the station right behind him. If I don't show, he'll come on his own," she lied, her voice scratchy. She needed to buy herself some time to think. "But it might take a few minutes."

Accepting that answer, Micah glanced over the puzzle. "What *is* this?"

"A logic puzzle," Lou whispered, but then something hit her. "Wait. You said you're not killers. What about Tyson, er, Cobra? You stabbed him in the barn."

It all made sense now. They'd called Willow to complain so she would find the body and wouldn't even consider them as suspects.

But then Rachel scoffed. "We did not."

"Daytona took care of that for us." Micah raised an eyebrow in challenge. "We told you, Lou. We're not killers. We used to steal cars, sure, but killing wasn't ever our intention. We didn't even really want to steal. When Chevelle got arrested, we tried to go straight, get jobs, do things right."

"But the right way was hard." Rachel wrinkled her nose. "So when Chev sent us the letters, we saw a way that we could live comfortably and get out of the country. And as long as that stab-happy freak, Daytona, doesn't ruin things for us tonight, we're going to be rich enough to start our lives in a different country, away from all this."

Lou almost sucked in a breath. Daytona. They didn't know he was Quincy, and they didn't know he was dead. They also didn't know that Quincy had an alibi for the night Tyson was stabbed in Willow's barn. A frown burrowed its way onto Lou's forehead.

If Rachel and Micah hadn't killed Tyson or Quincy, who had?

Fitz was in prison, and Bex Mason was … dead.

A cold sweat broke out across Lou's skin. Flashes of conversations jumped out at her:

Easton saying that the police weren't convinced Bex Mason had been Mustang.

"A lot of people get horse tattoos."

Fitz in his prison jumpsuit, cocking an eyebrow and saying, "And you think I'm the one who used violence?"

Gloria telling Lou that her son was the hot-wirer.

Wesley admitting that Doug's PI had been wrong about much of the stuff he researched.

Fitz's last message about Mustang. **If I had to face that person today, I'd run.** *Face them today. Because they weren't dead.*

Unhinged. Easton and Fitz had both used that word when describing the victims left over by the violent member of the Muscle Car Mafia.

Bex Mason wasn't Mustang.

"Oh, no." Lou's hands began shaking again.

"What?" Micah's face tightened.

A board creaked in the room above the garage. The master bedroom, Lou remembered from helping Easton move next door. All three of them froze, then glanced up.

"Please tell me you put Willow upstairs, and that was her moving up there," Lou whispered.

From the pale expressions on Rachel and Micah's faces, Lou knew the answer was not the one she'd hoped for.

That meant Mustang was here, ready to finish the job.

CHAPTER 24

Lou's eyes were wild as she raced toward the Ashleys.

Micah and Rachel weren't joking about not being violent because they didn't even stop her from snatching the puzzle from their fingers.

Shaking it in front of them, Lou whispered, "I made a mistake. Mustang isn't dead. Bex Mason wasn't Mustang. And now whoever is Mustang is here to take the two of you out, so you can't kill Easton before her, just like she did with Cobra and Daytona."

At the sound of Daytona's name on the list of those who'd been killed, Micah and Rachel shared a worried glance.

"You two need to come with me. Now. If we go to the police, they can protect you." Lou motioned to the open side door in the garage.

Rachel yanked her hand out of Lou's. "Are you mad? We're not going to the cops."

Lou gritted her teeth, hoping Mustang wasn't getting closer as they debated this. "Would you rather get in trouble for kidnapping or be dead at the hands of your most violent team-mate? Now, come on, we're wasting time. We have to run."

"Why do you care if we live?" Micah's eyes narrowed.

Lou's gaze snapped to him in her best angry New Yorker look. "Because you're the only people who know where my best friend is right now, and I need you to stay alive."

Another sound in the house startled them into reality. This time, it wasn't a creak but a stomping thump, like someone rushing down a set of stairs. Before Lou knew what was happening, the Ashleys were running toward the open garage side door. Lou didn't waste any time rushing after them. Once they were outside, Lou quickly passed the couple, leading the way down the driveway toward the police station.

But Mustang must've known she wouldn't be fast enough to catch up to them with that bad knee of hers because an engine revved behind them, and headlights illuminated the road. Tires squealed on the wet asphalt as a car came skidding around the corner by Easton's house, straight toward them. If Lou had to guess, she'd bet anything that Mustang had been driving the car that had almost run Easton off the road last week, prompting Willow to stay with Lou.

Lungs burning as she ran, Lou quickly realized they weren't going to make it.

"Ditch!" she yelled as the headlights grew behind them.

The three of them dove into the grassy ditch on the southern edge of Willow's property. The car swerved from left to right as Mustang worked to regain control after wrenching the wheel to the right, trying to hit them. She gunned the engine, heading down Pattern Drive.

For a split second, Lou thought she might be giving up, but then the car took an abrupt left onto Pin Street, the back end kicking out dirt and gravel as the tires squealed. She was going to loop back around.

And now, she was in between them and the police station.

Lou breathed deeply, arranging her thoughts into plans, then figuring out which plan had the lowest likelihood of death. Micah and Rachel scrambled to their feet next to her.

"Is she gone?" Micah asked through ragged, panting breaths.

Rachel groaned and grabbed her arm. She must've landed on it hard.

"Not gone. That road loops around." Eyes flashing to the other two with her, Lou said, "I think if we can do that again, we'll buy ourselves time to run to the station."

"Again?" Rachel whined.

"Yes," Lou said firmly. "If we can get her to come close once more, we can jump into this ditch again. Then when she's headed west down this road"—Lou gestured to their right, down the darker end of Thread Lane—"she won't have an easy turnaround. She'll either have to back up or do a three-point turn. While she does that, we run."

Micah and Rachel jerked their heads in frantic nods. Lou stepped into the road just as the sounds of the rumbly car engine and squealing tires grew closer. Headlights shone at the end of Pin Street.

But just as Mustang saw them in the street and gunned it toward them, a large truck raced down Pattern Drive.

Noah's truck.

Lou cried out, racing forward. The truck screeched to a halt sideways, blocking half of Pattern Drive and all of Thread Lane. The gears made a terrible grinding noise as Noah threw the truck into park. Lou's heart was in her throat as the sounds of Mustang's revving engine only grew louder as she continued to gun it toward the truck.

The truck's passenger side door flew open, and Lou almost cried out in relief as Noah jumped out. He ran toward her.

"Get out of the road," he called.

Now that he was out of the truck, Lou changed her direction. Instead of running toward Noah, she veered back toward the ditch. Tires screeched, and there was one last rev of the engine. Was Mustang trying to get around Noah's truck, or would she try to ram through it?

Just as Noah's arms wrapped around Lou, and they jumped toward the ditch, the terrible sound of metal crunching against metal and tires squealing rang out in the night. Lou's entire world was moving, like a bomb had gone off. Noah's truck skidded sideways down the road as Mustang ran straight into the side of it.

Lou's brain rattled as she hit the ground with an oomph.

Before she could get her bearings, Noah was hauling her to her feet, yelling something about running. Micah and Rachel were there too. Together, the four of them raced past the truck and toward the police station without looking back.

The officers were spilling out of the building as the foursome ran up to the station. The noise of the crash must've pulled them outside.

Easton raced to the front of the group. "What happened?"

"Mustang isn't dead." Lou panted out the words. "She tried to run us over."

"I'm on it." The even voice of the police chief cut through the chatter of officers. "Reynolds. Brenner. You're with me." A cruiser peeled out of the parking lot moments later, heading toward the site of the crash.

Noah's arms were around Lou as Easton rushed toward them.

"I don't understand. She came to my *old* house?" His gaze flicked to Micah and Rachel.

Remembering them, Lou noticed the two backing away from the group of officers ever so slowly.

"Oh, no. You two aren't going anywhere." Lou's wits returned, and she snapped into action. "Easton, meet Viper and Firebird, your renters." Lou glanced between the couple and Easton.

His expression darkened in realization, and the officers behind him immediately went for their guns, training them on the couple. Micah and Rachel held up their hands.

Easton's mouth hung open. "You two?" He coughed in confusion. "You rented my house so you could kill me?"

"Not technically." Lou raised her index finger in the air. "They say they didn't kill Cobra, and I believe them because they didn't even know Daytona was dead, or that he was Quincy. I think Mustang was the one who did all the killing."

Easton's attention flicked between his renters and Lou. "Then who has Willow?" The question was frayed at the edges.

Lou sucked in a breath. She forgot, that while she knew Willow was safe, Easton didn't. She was about to explain it all when Micah stepped forward.

"We took her. We thought we could use her as a bargaining chip to get you to cooperate during the parole hearing. That way no one had to die." Micah must've registered the deadly look Easton adopted at that information because he quickly added, "She's being kept in an old warehouse in Tinsdale. Don't worry. She's safe."

Easton didn't breathe a sigh of relief or show any signs of comfort. "Take me to her. Now."

Micah nodded quickly.

"Givens. Cuff Mrs. Ashley, please. The two of you are under arrest for kidnapping in the first degree." Easton released the cuffs from his belt and snapped them onto Micah's wrists as he read him his rights. Before they walked toward the cruiser, Easton looked at Lou and Noah. "Are you two going to be okay here?"

"We'll be fine," Noah assured him.

"Go get Willow," Lou said, her voice wobbling with emotion.

Easton gave her a small smile. Moments later, Officer Givens and Easton drove away with Rachel and Micah in the back, heading toward Tinsdale. The remaining officers moved back inside, calling out to Lou and Noah that they could join them.

Lou finally met Noah's eyes. She placed her hands on either side of his face and leaned up to kiss him.

"Thank you," she whispered. "Also, how did you know where we were?" The volume of her voice grew. "And your truck!" She groaned. "It's probably totaled."

Noah leaned forward to pull her into a hug. "You texted me to stay put, but I worried when I didn't hear from you. I got in my truck and was just crossing Spool when I saw that maniac try to run you and two other people over. I didn't think about my truck. I just knew I had to block that car from getting to you, and it seemed like the best option." He huffed a soft laugh into her hair.

Lou kissed him again, hugging him tight to her. "I'm not sure acts of chivalry are covered under insurance."

Noah smiled. "I needed a new truck anyway. That one was twice as old as Marigold."

They were about to go inside when Officer Brenner came running back to the station on foot. The lights and sirens of an ambulance raced down Thread Lane toward the sight of the accident.

"Everything okay?" Lou asked.

Brenner nodded, breathing hard as he came to a stop in front of them. "She hit her head on the steering wheel in the crash. She's pretty banged up. They're taking her to the hospital. Chief told me to come back here and get your statement, Lou. That way, he can be ready to charge her when she wakes up."

Lou followed Brenner as he led the way into the station, more than happy to comply with that request. She wanted whomever Mustang was to get exactly what she deserved.

CHAPTER 25

Willow sighed as she closed the stall door. If OC's joyous whinnies and Steve's aggressive bleating were any indication, the two were ecstatic to be back home. They relaxed right into the barn after taking a quick turn around the paddock, as if checking to make sure everything was still the same.

A smile took over Willow's face for the first time in a week. She leaned her weight into the stall. Lou closed the bin where Willow kept the animals' supplements, and she sat on the lid.

"Things feeling right with the universe again?" Lou asked.

"Better." She dipped her chin. "Still not perfect, but getting there."

"What's feeling unfinished to you?" Lou wondered if there were still loose ends for her friend when it came to the attempts on Easton's life or her abduction the other day.

But Willow didn't mention the case. "Now we're back at

square one with renters. We'll have to go through applications and interviews again, when all I want to do is sleep for about a month straight."

Lou had been right that her friend hadn't been getting restful sleep during the week and a half Easton's life had been at risk. The dark circles under her eyes gave her away even more.

Pushing herself off the wall with a grunt, Willow gestured for Lou to follow her inside. "Want some hot chocolate while we wait for George to get here?"

"Always." As much as Lou loved hanging out in the cozy barn, she was happy to be returning to the even warmer house, especially if hot beverages were being supplied. It was Tuesday, and Willow had asked to have their weekly girls' night at her house that week so she could make sure OC and Steve were settling in okay from their trip home.

Before they could reach the porch, the sound of footsteps crunching through the frozen grass caused them to stop and peer around the house. George rounded into the backyard, her expression perking up at the sight of them.

"Hey, I knocked, but figured you were in the barn."

Willow opened the sliding glass door and motioned for them to enter.

They spent the next few minutes making drinks, plating appetizers, and getting a movie queued on the screen. Once they were situated on the couch, Willow picked up the remote control and pointed it at the television.

Lou cleared her throat. "Hold on. Before we start, there's a piece of business we have to take care of."

Willow's eyebrows rose. George blinked.

"How did your second date with Josh go?" Lou asked. "You said it was last night, right?"

"It's *Jason*," George said through a laugh, but then the young woman's cheeks flushed, and her gaze dropped to her lap. "I, uh, there wasn't one."

"Wait. Why?" Willow's legs, which had been tucked underneath her in preparation for the movie, snapped out as if she might jump into action and go hunt down this Jason guy.

George held up a hand to stop her, and she shot a placating smile at Lou. "It's for the best. I promise. He called me this weekend and told me that he and his ex had patched things up, and he didn't want to string me along." George swallowed. "The day I heard from him was when that terrible Mustang lady woke up, and you guys were preoccupied, so I didn't bring it up."

Mustang had woken up after being out for a full twenty-six hours. Her name was Vera Steig, and she was currently being charged with double homicide and attempted vehicular homicide.

She'd been uncooperative, but that didn't matter because Rachel and Micah Ashley were more than happy to help, if it meant a lighter sentence for them. They handed over all the proof Easton needed to link Chevelle to the contract on his life.

Lou had to admit Willow and Easton had been pretty distracted that day, as had she. She didn't blame George for keeping the news about her dating life to herself.

Relaxing back in her chair, Lou said, "I'm sorry, George. That's still hard, even if you can see that it's for the best."

"It's okay. I'll have to accept that Geralt might be the only man in my life for the foreseeable future." She laughed.

Willow glanced sidelong at Lou, sipping her cocoa to hide the look.

"I saw the movers came to take the Ashleys' stuff away," George told Willow.

"Ugh. Don't remind me." Willow groaned. "I was just telling Lou that I'd almost rather have kidnappers next door than have to go through the process of finding new renters. Though, it would be hard to get the image of them pulling up outside the bookstore that night, calling me over, and telling me they were going to kill Easton if I didn't come quietly with them, out of my nightmares if they were still next door." She shivered.

Lou sat up straight, jolted forward like an electric shock had moved through her body. It had, in a way, in the form of an idea.

"What?" Willow's expression morphed into one of hope.

"Noah."

George blinked.

"Yeah," Willow said. "What about him?"

"What if he moved into your rental?" Lou asked, quickly adding, "He's not having any luck finding a new place of his own. You know him, so you wouldn't have to worry about criminals moving in next door again, and he's very tidy, so you know he'd take care of the place."

Willow exhaled a wry laugh. "Why didn't I think of that before?" She slapped the heel of her hand onto her forehead. "You're right. It's perfect. Do you think Noah would want to live that close to us?"

"I don't see why not." Lou bounced her shoulders in a quick shrug. "It's way more land than he's got right now in that cramped neighborhood. And he loves you and Easton."

Willow settled back onto the couch. "Okay, *now* I can officially relax. Thanks, Lou."

Lou smirked. "Anytime."

And with that, Willow started the movie.

WHEN NOAH CAME by the bookshop the following day, during lunch, Lou's first reaction was to smile at the surprise visit. But that grin fell as she noticed his tense posture and the way his hands were shoved stiffly into his pockets.

"Hey," she said warily. "Is everything okay?"

Oh no, she thought with a flash of worry. *He was being nice on the phone last night when I called and suggested that he rent Easton's house. He doesn't want to, and he feels like I'm forcing him into it.*

"I'm sorry," she blurted.

Noah's head jutted back in surprise. Confusion and humor flashed in his hazel eyes. "For what?" he asked.

"For forcing the issue of you renting Easton's place. It was pushy, and I'll call Willow right now to tell her you can't do it."

Tilting his head to one side, Noah asked, "What makes you think I don't want to rent Easton's house? I told you last night that I think it's a great idea."

His sincerity made her stumble. "Well, you look all tense and nervous, and I thought you didn't know how to tell me no. We haven't exactly had a ton of fights yet in our relationship, and I figured you were nervous because you didn't know how I'd react."

Noah's face lit up with a dimpled smile. "I'm nervous and

tense, Louisa Henry, because I came here to ask you if you'll move into Easton's house with me, not because I don't think it's a good idea. And we haven't had many fights in our relationship yet because you're the most level-headed, thoughtful person I've ever met."

Surprise jolted through Lou. She opened her mouth, but nothing came out.

Stepping forward, Noah grinned down at her. "I know we've only been together for six months, but I don't need longer to know that you're it for me, Lou."

"What about Marigold?" Lou scrunched her forehead together.

"It was her idea." He laughed. "Well, not *only* hers. I was thinking it after you called last night, but she was the one who voiced it first."

Lou considered that. She'd known Marigold was there with Noah last night, having heard her call out a hello when Noah told her who was on the phone.

"What about the cats?" Lou glanced around at the bookshop fosters.

"Them being alone here during the evenings is about the same as people who leave their cats at home while they go to work each day. *But* if you want, we can put a bunch of crates in your car and you can bring them back and forth with you each day you come to work."

Lou tried to picture that but ended up chuckling and cringing. "Maybe just Sapphire, if he seems like he's missing me." Wetting her lips, Lou said, "Live next door to my best friend?" The question was a whisper, a fantasy.

"Live next door to *our* best friends," Noah corrected. "With enough space for Marigold to have her own room, two spare rooms in case your brother-in-law and his family come to visit, and space for your parents to park their RV anytime." He beamed.

Lou laughed, joy making her feel as light as air. "Yes, of course I will."

Noah picked her up, spinning her around in a circle as he kissed her. He checked his watch and said, "Okay, I've got an appointment to get back to, but dinner tonight?"

"Sure." Lou beamed. "Oh, wait. I promised Gloria I'd stop by and help her tonight."

"Then dinner with Gloria tonight, it is." Noah winked. "I'll pick you up around five so we can grab ingredients at the store."

Lou's heart felt like it might burst. "See you then."

With that, Noah jogged out the door and back toward the veterinary clinic. Lou found Sapphy, scooping her cat into her arms and hugging him tight as she smiled into his fur. The white cat blinked his impossibly blue eyes at her in question, but purred at the attention nonetheless. When she was done celebrating with him, Lou brought out her phone to call Willow.

When Lou told her the good news, the squeal Willow let out in response was loud enough that Lou had to hold the phone at a distance. Mr. Clawrcy and Jane Pawsten, who'd been cuddling together on the love seat, lifted their heads and blinked. Once they realized the sound had stopped, they tucked themselves back into a perfect heart shape and went back to sleep.

Book 10 - Dangerous Infurmation

Can't they have a *meowment* of peace?

A rise in shoplifting has Button and its neighboring cities on edge. Lou, whose bookstore was the first business targeted, is eager to figure out how to stop the thieves. Before they can, Lou's neighboring business owner is killed during a robbery gone wrong.

Desperate to seek justice for her neighbor, Lou can't help but get involved. She dives headfirst into the investigation, determined to unravel the chilling agenda behind the crimes. As secrets unravel and dark motives come to light, the shocking truth threatens to shake Button to its very core. Will Lou uncover the sinister truth before it's too late?

Get Your Copy!

Join Eryn Scott's mailing list to learn about new releases and sales!

ALSO BY ERYN SCOTT

STONEYBROOK MYSTERIES

Ongoing series * Farmers market * Recipes * Crime solving twins * Cats!

A MURDER AT THE MORRISEY MYSTERY SERIES

Ongoing series * Friendly ghosts * Quirky downtown Seattle building

Pebble Cove Teahouse Mysteries

Completed series * Friendly ghosts * Oregon Coast * Cat mayors

Whiskers and Words Mysteries

Ongoing series * Best friends *
Bookshop full of cats

PEPPER BROOKS
COZY MYSTERY SERIES

Completed series * Literary mysteries * Sweet romance * Cute dog

About the Author

Eryn Scott lives in the Pacific Northwest with her husband and their quirky animals. She loves classic literature, musicals, knitting, and hiking. She writes cozy mysteries and women's fiction.

Join her mailing list to learn about new releases and sales!

www.erynscott.com